BU
TREA

Alan Scholefield

HEADLINE

First published in 1995
by HEADLINE BOOK PUBLISHING

10 9 8 7 6 5 4 3 2 1

British Library Cataloguing in Publication Data

Scholefield, Alan
Buried Treasure
I.Title
823.914 [F]

ISBN 0 7472 1144 2

Typeset by Avon Dataset Ltd, Bidford-on-Avon, B50 4JH

Printed and bound in Great Britain by
Mackays of Chathams Plc, Chatham, Kent

HEADLINE BOOK PUBLISHING
A division of Hodder Headline PLC
338 Euston Road,
London NW1 3BH

ACKNOWLEDGEMENTS

My thanks for his help go, as usual, to Dr Robin Ilbert of the Prison Service. Any mistakes are my own.

1

There had never been a killing in that place.

That's what they said.

They were wrong, of course.

Two hundred and eleven years ago a husband murdered his wife for sleeping with his groom. Then, for good measure, he killed the groom.

If you go back far enough there's been a murder in most places.

This one happened only months ago.

People in the village said it was 'unbelievable', 'horrendous', 'ghastly', 'dreadful'. In 1784 the words had been 'vengeful', 'baleful' and 'sorrowful'.

Same village, different people.

In those days the village was described as 'Stepttone near Kingstoune in the Countie of Sussex'. Nowadays it is called Stepton and has a post code.

Then, it had a square and a population of peasants. It had a church, two alehouses, a forge, a washhouse, a small workhouse and a large grave-yard.

Today the squire's place is held by an elderly woman who lives alone in the big house. The church which was the centre of all village life is used only on alternate Sundays. The two alehouses are now converted into smart village pubs, and the workhouse has been turned into a nursing home for the old. A forge still operates but no longer shoes horses, instead the blacksmith spends his time making wrought-iron gates and *objets d'art*. The graveyard has grown smaller and neater, for the peasants aren't buried their any longer. Indeed, there are no peasants and the few farm workers remaining, who live in council houses, would feel insulted to be thus described.

No, Stepton is a modern English village, part retirement home, part dormitory suburb for London commuters, and part, a tiny part, still devoted to the land that surrounds it.

It lies aside the River Step – full of brown trout and some rainbows – and is very beautiful.

Once the commuters leave in the morning it falls into a tranquil doze until they return in the evening.

American tourists call it timeless.

The English call it fashionable.

In his summing-up to the jury in Regina v Mason Chitty, Mr Justice Stackhouse called it a murderous place.

2

'... and so, members of the jury, I must remind you of the severity of the charge. Murder is the most serious crime our courts normally hear.'

Mr Justice Stackhouse used his black and shiny fountain pen to mark off with a tick the point he had just made, then he drew breath and said, 'Now we come to the problem of the body, or lack of it. And you may think that this is the most important factor. Certainly the defence has made that point and I shall only paraphrase it: how, they ask you, can you find the defendant guilty when the young woman he is alleged to have killed has never been found?'

The afternoon sun was streaming through the high windows of Number One court in Kingstown and the air was close and hot on this late spring day. Earlier, His Lordship, a large and florid man, had asked for the windows to be opened but the long poles used to pull down the catches could not be found and Number One court, which until twenty odd years ago was called an Assize Court and is now called a Crown Court, did not have air conditioning. Indeed it had few modern amenities, dating as it did from the early part of the eighteenth

3

century and containing in the dust and the grease on its walls particles of justice and injustice handed down over the centuries.

It was said that Judge Jeffreys had sat here soon after the Bloody Assizes and certainly hundreds of people had been sentenced, if not to death, at least to Australia. Dickens could have known a courtroom like it, perhaps he had even seen his father sentenced in a similar room. It would be familiar to anyone who has read *Bleak House*.

Today it was a sweaty and dismal place, especially for the accused.

Mr Justice Stackhouse said, 'The question of the missing victim has been most exhaustively examined by both the defence and the prosecution. The prosecution's case is that Miss Benson was murdered callously and brutally and the body disposed of.

'We have heard evidence that in spite of an intensive search by the police who used the most modern equipment, no trace of Miss Benson has been found.

'We know what the defence has made of this but it is countered by the prosecution with medical evidence as to the blood which was found on the accused.

'Ladies and gentlemen, you have heard a great deal of medical evidence. Some of it has been highly technical and I do not wish to burden you with more, but inevitably we come to one aspect above all others: the question of DNA. Now you have heard precisely what DNA is and it is not for me to enlarge upon that. Suffice it to say that DNA is a kind of blood fingerprint and the prosecution has led evidence to show that a small amount of blood with Miss Benson's unique DNA, in other words her personal fingerprint, was found upon the accused.'

The courtroom was packed and several women were fanning themselves with pieces of paper. In the third row of the onlookers sat Henry Vernon, an elderly four-square man with a damp, bald head. Next to him was his daughter Anne, thirtyish, good-looking, and slightly taller than her father.

'Goodness, he does go on,' Henry Vernon said in a loud aside.

'Keep your voice down,' Anne hissed.

'There's nothing wrong with my voice.' Henry had taken off his jacket and his bare arms were short and muscular. His small white moustache highlighted the ruddiness of his face. Although he was perspiring freely he was comfortable in the heat. Most of his adult life had been spent in parts of Africa where he had dispensed the Queen's justice as prosecutor and later as judge in the Colonial Service. He had occupied the bench – metaphorically speaking – in tin huts, in grass huts, in brick huts, under mopani trees and under corrugated iron roofs so hot you could have fried mutton chops on them, so to him, Number One court in Kingstown was just cosily warm.

Fearful that he might go on talking, Anne moved as far away from him as her seat would allow. This did not achieve the desired effect for he said of the judge, 'I've heard him before, he's a bloody bore.'

A woman sitting in a seat ahead of him half turned. She was older than Henry – in her seventies – small and thin, and looked frail until you looked more closely. There was something about the disapproving set of the eyes and the jaw that made people uneasy. Her expression was unforgiving and her body seemed to be made of steel wire.

Mr Justice Stackhouse said: 'You have heard expert witnesses declare that the blood found on the accused was that of Sandra Benson, the murdered girl . . .'

Henry glared round the courtroom. 'Who are all these people anyway?' he said.

'Villagers,' Anne said. 'Not so loud.'

'All of them?'

'How am I supposed to know?'

'I thought you knew everything.'

The woman in front of Henry looked round again. Anne knew she was Florence Chitty, the mother of the accused man, Mason Chitty. By her side was her other son, Samuel. They had occupied the same seats since the trial began. And she could see, across the courtroom, another major player in the case, Mrs Lily Benson, the mother of the murdered girl – or at least the girl the prosecution alleged had been murdered. She was a big woman who would normally have been handsome. Now her face was shrivelled and white. She looked down at her hands and for a moment Anne thought she was going to cry, but she managed to hold back her tears.

'. . . and so, ladies and gentlemen, according to what we know – and we know very little about those moments other than what the accused has told us himself – we must try to come to a decision . . .'

'Oh get on with it!' Henry said, and Anne shifted away from him again.

'. . . we have heard that blood was found on the accused's watch strap and also under his fingernails. Both, according to the medical experts, belonged to Miss Benson, and this was not challenged by the defence.'

In shifting her position Anne had placed herself unwittingly where it was easier to see Mason Chitty and as she looked up at him she caught his eyes. He was sitting in the box with a prison officer on either side of him as he had been for the duration of the trial. He was dressed in much the same way as he had dressed in prison: a tattersall checked shirt, a school tie, a tweed sports jacket and grey trousers.

His eyes held hers and she saw in them the same mute appeal she was familiar with. She smiled and he nodded and tried to smile in return, then he looked down at his hands. She had to remind herself that he was in his forties, not his fifties.

'... so what are we to make of this story?' Mr
Justice Stackhouse asked the jury. 'The accused
has said he was having an affair with Miss Benson.
He has said that they were in the habit of
performing the sexual act in the stables on his farm,
that on this occasion she was menstruating and
that is how her blood came to be found upon him.

'I do not propose to discuss the likelihood of this
occurring, you will have your own thoughts. And I
must remind you that there is no agreement
between prosecution and defence experts as to
whether this was menstrual blood or not.'

Anne looked at the clock. It was going on for
noon, Mr Justice Stackhouse had been talking
for nearly two hours and she wanted him to finish.
She had come to court because Mason Chitty had
asked her to. Then her father had said he would
be attending too. He spent a great deal of his
time these days in courtrooms, not employed to be
there but because, she was sure, he had a terri-
torial feeling since he had spent all his adult life in
them.

And of course they offered him an escape from
his daily life. For who would have thought – who
could possibly ever have imagined – that Judge
Henry Vernon, who once had huge areas of Africa
under his judicial control, would end up sharing a
house with his daughter in a cathedral city in the
south of England, doing the household shopping
and some of the cooking, as well as looking after

8

his granddaughter, Hilly, like some strangely aberrant au pair?

In all her childhood Anne could never remember him doing anything of a domestic nature. His food had arrived on the table without him knowing or wanting to know whence it came, his clothes had appeared washed and ironed and ready to put on. And when Anne's mother had left them and done a bolt back to England, they were looked after by the peerless Watch, part legal clerk, part valet, part major domo and part friend. Watch did no domestic work either. That was attended to by servants. But he watched the servants.

Anne's and Henry's lives had been controlled by Watch for many years. Eventually Anne had gone to England for her education and become a doctor. Henry had stayed on in Africa and used his knowledge of the law to help emerging nations to create their new judiciaries. It was only when he retired to the Cape of Good Hope and then became so ill that Anne wanted him to return to England that the partnership with Watch broke up. Henry had a pacemaker fitted in London and Watch went back to live in Lesotho with his widowed sister and her family.

His Lordship's voice went on and on. Anne glanced again at Mason Chitty. His face was a dirty white against the dark mahogany of the dock. He was leaning forward, his head resting on his hand. He had sat like that in her room in the prison hospital the day before his trial was to start and had said, 'Please . . . please . . . Dr Vernon . . . don't let them do this to me . . .'

And she had said, 'There's nothing I can do to stop them, Mason.'

'Surely you above all people must have a doubt. You must question whether I did it or not.'

'Mason, I've told you before, I can only answer medico-legal questions. There really isn't anything more I can do.'

It had been terrible to hear the grief in his voice.

Her boss, Tom Melville, had said, 'Don't let it get to you. *There's nothing you can do.*'

Even as she used his phrase to Chitty she had felt ashamed, for she knew quite well what Tom was referring to. When she had first joined the prison service and begun work in the Kingstown prison hospital she had winced at what seemed to her Tom's brutally uninvolved approach to the prisoners who came to them with physical or mental problems. But she had soon learnt to copy him, for there were just too many problems and coping with them all was like loading herself with endless pieces of other people's luggage.

Until Jameson, that is. She tried not to think about Jameson.

'May I?' a voice said.

Anne looked up to see an elderly woman waiting to get past her to a vacant seat. Henry rose too, his face registering his disapproval of being disturbed.

The woman was dressed in a flowing dress in sombre grey that was so out of fashion as to be almost fashionable. Her crocodile-skin handbag was large and worn but Anne guessed it must originally have cost a fortune. This was the impression the woman gave, of someone who had once been worth a fortune, and was now down on her luck. And there was something about her face . . . then Anne knew who she was, for photographs of most of the Stepton villagers had been in the papers since the trial had begun. This surely was Mrs Drayton, the *grande dame* who—

There was a sudden cry. A muffled shout. Uproar. People were on their feet. The Clerk of the Court was banging his gavel and calling for silence. The judge leaned forward to see what was going on.

Anne rose, then an usher caught her arm.

'Quickly, doctor!'

He led her through a crowd of people to the dock. The two prison officers were with Mason Chitty. He had fallen off his chair and while one of the officers was trying to ease him into a semi-recumbent position with his back to the interior wall of the dock the other was handcuffing himself to Chitty's right arm.

'What happened?' Anne said.

'Don't know, doc. He just fell off the chair.'

The court was cleared as she examined Mason. She was getting a high pulse rate, but otherwise he seemed in reasonable shape.

One of the officers said, 'Can we take him down, doc?'

'All right,' she said. 'I'll get my bag.'

They lifted Chitty and took him down into the cells below the courtroom. As Anne was going out to her car Mrs Chitty blocked her path.

'Are you pleased now?' she said.

Samuel, dark and saturnine, stared at Anne. She brushed past them as the judge, barristers and court officials waited.

When she returned from the cells she said, 'He's not fit for trial, m'lud.'

Mr Justice Stackhouse adjourned the hearing and admonished the jury not to discuss it with each other or with anyone else, and by anyone else he meant especially the media.

3

On a warm spring day Kingstown was at its best. It was still too early in the season for the cathedral close to be crowded by tourists, and residents were able to walk the narrow streets in the old part of the town without being photographed.

Dwellings had been built in this place on the south slope of the Downs even before the Romans came to Britain. When they did arrive they built a fortified village. Tiles and coins have been found and the remains of a villa with a hypocaust.

It is a rich city and a beautiful one, marred only slightly by the classic Victorian prison which, with the ruins of a medieval castle, dominates the skyline.

Beneath the castle is a long-stay car-park and Lily Benson stood for a moment trying to recall where she had left her car. Not only could she not remember parking, she could not remember driving there, and it took her several minutes to find her small Toyota.

She drove through the warm, attractive streets and out into the countryside where the ash and oak trees were in full leaf.

The blank in her mind where the car had been

13

was echoed by another blank. When the court hearing had been adjourned she had wandered aimlessly through the city streets but for how long she did not know. This frightened her. Parts of her life were now regularly missing.

It was mid-afternoon when she reached Stepton. As she drove into the village it presented itself to her symbolically. On the outskirts was a group of ugly council houses, at the centre were the beautiful Queen Anne and Georgian dwellings of the original village, and between the two was a buffer of houses put up by a speculative builder in 1964. Hers was one of these. It was not nearly as good as the old graceful village houses but better than the council houses, and this reflected the attitudes of the villagers.

'We won't be here long,' her husband had said when they moved in. 'We'll live above the pub.'

That had been the plan. A pub in the south of England. Pub-keeper. Publican. Mine host. Barry had used those phrases often; sometimes with a little laugh. But he'd believed them. That's how he had seen himself: as mine host.

They had spent the last six years of his Navy contract planning their future, dreaming of it.

Barry had come up from the lower deck and ended as a lieutenant. His father had been a refuse collector so he'd started the hard way, at the bottom.

My God, she had thought when he was promoted, I'm married to an officer.

Of course there were officers and officers, but if Barry was on a slightly different level from those who had graduated from naval colleges, what the hell? He was an officer.

But what he really wanted to be was a pub-keeper and the pub he wanted was on a trout stream. One day, some months after he had left the navy, he'd found it – the Mayfly on the River Step in Stepton.

He'd signed a tenancy agreement with the brewery that owned it and he and Lily and Sandra had moved into temporary accommodation in Stepton.

Then, before they could take over the pub, he'd died. Just like that. Heart attack. Only in his forties. It happened that way sometimes, the doctor had said. Lily and Sandra had stayed on in Stepton.

She parked the car in a small lane at the back of her house and let herself in. To anyone else the place would have appeared spotless. To her it seemed dirty and dusty. She began to clean. She cleaned the kitchen first, then the bathroom, then the living-room. She went back into the kitchen and pulled out the stove and cleaned the skirting board behind it. She had not cleaned it for a couple of days. Pulling out the stove left dirty marks on the vinyl floor so she cleaned that too.

As she cleaned she wept. These were the tears she had held back in court. Now she could cry, for they were tears for Sandra and this was Sandra's home.

She cleaned and cleaned and the light began to go out of the day. Evening came, and still she cleaned. She had not told the doctor she did this because she was worried about what he might think. She hadn't told him about the memory blanks either.

Because she knew what was happening to her. Even though she could not stop it she knew *why*. Or thought she did.

'And so do you, my darling,' she said to Sandra.

It was time for Sandra now.

She put away the cleaning things and went up to her daughter's room. It was just as though Sandra had gone out to the pub or the shop. Not a thing had been changed or moved.

It was a blue room. Blue and pink. On the bed was a big Pluto, and inside Pluto were Sandra's beautiful silk pyjamas. Every week Lily washed them and ironed them and put them back, as if Sandra was on holiday somewhere and would be coming home in a few days.

There was one change: the kitchen chair Lily had placed in the centre of the pink-and-blue carpet. She sat on the chair because nothing on God's earth would have made her sit on Sandra's bed and disturb it.

'Hello, my darling,' she said to Sandra's

photograph, which stood on the bedside table. 'You know what happened today? He collapsed in the dock. Fell off his chair. They've stopped the case until he's well again. I don't mind, it makes it worse for him and that's what counts.'

She began to tidy the room and as she did so she went on talking.

She told Sandra about the courtroom scenes and then asked her what she'd like for her supper. Chilli? Fish fingers? Beefburgers? No . . . she didn't have any beefburgers and she didn't want to go to the shop to buy some.

'They'd only ask about the case, and I don't want to talk to them about it.'

She talked to Sandra for more than an hour, then she went downstairs. The late-evening sun was just dipping behind the beech trees on the hill that marked the boundary of 'the farm'. She didn't like to call it by its name and never called the owners by their name – not when she was talking to Sandra. It was just 'the farm' and 'them', and 'him'.

Somewhere . . . somewhere over there, they said that Sandra lay buried. For a long time she had simply not accepted that thought. Sandra wasn't dead so how could she be buried? But when Sandra's blood was found on 'him' she had had to change her thoughts. In the depths of her mind she knew that her daughter was never coming back. Like Barry. But often she didn't – couldn't – accept what she knew. She tried and frequently succeeded in living in the surface layer of her mind and then she didn't have to accept it.

She stood at the window but now saw nothing except the fresh face of her daughter. It was everywhere: in the window glass; above the stove; in the water of the sink.

The tears came again. She went through to the living-room and sat in her chair.

A whole evening stretched ahead of her.

Days . . . weeks . . . months . . .

The future terrified her.

She closed her eyes.

And then Sandra spoke to her.

Find me, she said.

'Right, let's have it,' Stimson said. 'How did he get the stuff?'

Anne and Tom Melville, the prison's senior medical officer, were in the governor's rooms. The suite was in the admin section. There was an office for his secretary, an office for himself and a boardroom with a table and eight chairs. The three were seated round the table.

Roger Stimson was a heavily jowled man with blue-black hair going grey at the temples, and hairy hands. By late afternoon each day he needed another shave. People who met him thought he looked jovial for a prison governor until they noticed that his eyes looked as though they could penetrate case-hardened steel.

18

'Where?' Stimson said.

'The usual,' Tom said. 'Health-care staff. Jenks says Chitty complained of chronic headaches. He dished out the paracetamol as and when.'

The governor shook his head angrily. 'He was in the hospital a lot of the time and your people let him do it!'

Tom rose and went to the window, walking with little, jerky movements. He was in his thirties, tall with black hair unfashionably long and when he spoke he moved arms and hands and sometimes his whole body. He seemed filled with an enormous reservoir of untapped energy. He turned from the windows and said, 'That's what you want, isn't it?'

'What I want? What the hell are you talking about?'

'Home Office policy. Let the prisoners develop more responsibility for their lives by taking their pills when they want to.'

'Jesus, I didn't advocate any such bloody policy, I've said it a thousand times.'

'But you're the symbolic representative of such policy.'

Anne was always surprised at the sharp tone Tom took with Stimson. Yet the two of them got on well enough. She had decided that Tom acted the way he did because he really didn't care one way or the other if he continued working in the prison service and the governor knew it. He also knew he'd never get another doctor as good as Tom.

Stimson lit a cigarette and waved the smoke away from the two doctors.

'I'll tell you something,' he said. 'It may be Home Office policy to let prisoners take bathroom-cupboard drugs in their own time in private but it's also Home Office policy that prisoners mustn't kill themselves. If Chitty dies – how long will he be on the danger list, anyway?'

'Nearly three weeks.'

'Well, if he dies what is going to land on me will land from a dizzy height. And then I'm going to make some of it land on your outfit because that's where it should land, especially after Jameson, comprendo?'

'He's not going to try again,' Tom said. 'We've got him in a safe room. I'm not even sure he meant to kill himself.'

'What's that supposed to mean?'

Anne said, 'Tom thinks it might just have been delaying tactics.'

'Why? I mean he doesn't know if he's going to be found guilty. He might even get off. What makes you so confident he won't?'

'The girl's DNA,' Tom said.

'She might have been having her period like he says,' Stimson said. 'And even if he's found guilty there'll probably be an appeal.'

The three looked at each other in silence.

Anne was exhausted. She had been in court on

and off for the past week but still had a big work load. It was now late afternoon and she had spent the past few hours getting Mason Chitty to hospital, having his stomach emptied of paracetamol, then returning him to the prison hospital.

The governor said, 'If that bloody TV outfit gets wind of this things will begin to fly even if Chitty doesn't try to top himself.'

'I think he will,' Anne said.

'What?'

'Have another go. Try to kill himself.'

Stimson said, 'Why?'

'I think he's probably innocent.'

'Oh, Jesus,' Stimson said. 'We couldn't live with another Jameson.'

They talked for another half an hour and when they left Stimson's rooms Tom said to Anne, 'Fancy a drink?'

She shook her head, 'I want to see Mason and then I've got to pick up Hilly. Can I have a raincheck?'

'Do you really think he'll try again?'

'Maybe. What would happen if he succeeded?'

'You heard Roger. He'd make us suffer a bit and I wouldn't like that.'

She started to ask him the obvious question and then closed her mouth. The thought of him not being there was like a sudden cold wind.

They walked back through the yard where the great walls of the Victorian House of Correction reared up. Even higher than the walls were the thin steel cables that intersected the air above large empty spaces. At first Anne had been unable to guess what these wires were for and Tom had explained they were to stop helicopters being used in escape attempts. Now, even though she might not have guessed their exact purpose, she would have known they were there for something special. Nothing was added to or subtracted from Kingstown prison for fun.

They went into her room which still bore the pale-green paint with which the prison had thought fit to decorate the room of its first female doctor. It had been Tom's choice and even though pale-green was not her favourite colour she had been touched that such niceties were observed in an all-male prison where the prevailing colours were cream and brown.

'Tea?' she said.

'Coffee would be better, I need the caffeine.'

He sat in the chair opposite her desk, the one on which the prisoners would sit when they came to discuss their mental problems – their physical problems were usually discussed at the morning surgery which took place in the main block. The hospital was a small modern unit which stood on its own with private rooms, a ward, a laboratory and an X-ray room.

Tom sipped his coffee and said, 'Roger's right about Chitty. If he does top himself we'll all be on

the TV news, you can bet on that. I wonder if he's
ever tried before?'

'Suicide? There's not a hint of it in the
psychiatrists' reports. Ah . . . but you never really
believe them do you?'

'Not as though they're tablets of stone, anyway,
I've read too many that were flawed.' He rose and
began his familiar pacing. 'There's a report that
says that since patients have been released from
the secure hospitals as part of the care-in-the-
community programme, they've committed an
average of one murder a month. And *they* were
released on the basis of psychiatrists' reports.'

She let this go. 'His mother and his brother never
look at him in court.'

'What sort of a family are they?'

'Farmers. Well heeled, I'm told.'

'Will they go to the media?'

'Why should they?'

'Lack of a corpse is always good copy.'

'From what I've seen of them and heard about
them they wouldn't give a reporter the time of
day.'

He finished his coffee. 'Well, if you're not going
to come and have a drink with me, I'm off.'

He went to the door.

'How's Beanie?' she said.

'She's fine. Jumping onto chairs again.'

'Hilly was asking.'

'Bring her out. Tell her I've found a new

23

American ice-cream. It's called Smith and Wesson, or some such name.'

Find me!
Did she say that?
Yes, I'm here! I'll find you, darling. Just tell me where you are.
Lily is freezing yet the house is warm.
I must find her, she says aloud to the listening walls.
I will ... I'll find you ...
But where?
She looks out into the gathering dusk.
The farm fills the evening sky. The house is on the top of the small hill, lights shine in the windows.
Find me ...
Yes, my love, I'll find you.
Where does Sandra's voice come from?
Has she dreamt it? Is she dreaming now?
She pinches herself and feels it.
No dream.
Then the voice comes again ...

4

Henry Vernon, BA, LLB (Cantab), barrister-at-law and former judge, was boiling an egg. Since he had lost the services of Watch and become what he called, with a mixture of contempt and irony, a 'house-mother', he had had to do a certain amount of cooking.

In the old Africa days he had often wandered out with a shotgun and brought back a brace of guinea-fowl for the pot, the cooking of which was overseen by Watch. A similar situation could not obtain in Kingstown.

One of the dishes Watch had himself cooked and of which Henry had never tired, was smoked haddock boiled gently in milk and accompanied by a poached egg on toast. Watch would make this outstanding dish on a fire of dried cow dung – also a problem to find in Kingstown.

For a reason which Henry had not been able to fathom, his granddaughter, for whom he cooked regularly – and his daughter too, for that matter – did not seem to have the same appetite for smoked haddock as he had.

'Tins,' he had said to Anne one day, 'that's all you people think about. No one cooks a proper meal any longer. I mean, all that prepared stuff in the supermarkets, it can't do you much good.'

When she had pointed out that he had never in his whole life cooked a proper meal he had been somewhat offended.

So now he was learning. He had come across a small book called *Nice Things to Eat* which seemed to be aimed at the young. It was exactly what he needed because he was cooking for the young.

He was now cooking eggs 'in the flamenco style' – with some minor modifications of his own. The book called for small baking dishes in which the eggs and a tomato mixture were supposed to cook in the oven.

What did small baking dishes look like? He vaguely knew he had seen large metal ones in which bread was baked, so whoever had written the book clearly had got it wrong. Baking dishes were not small.

A misprint perhaps?

An excellent variation would be to hardboil the eggs and then cover them with a good dollop of tomato ketchup. It wasn't quite the sauce the book advocated but children liked tomato ketchup.

So . . . he was boiling eggs.

Anne's kitchen, where he was working, was on the ground floor of their Georgian house. Henry lived in the basement flat. Kingstown had more Georgian houses than any other English city of its size. Neither he nor Anne would ever have been able to afford the house individually, but together they had.

And Henry had not been sorry. Although he thought Britain in the 1990s was a dismal place of rampant capitalism on the one hand and voracious socialism on the other – each devouring the other – he had to admit that it was better than many countries he knew where the panga and the AK 47 ruled.

He heard the front door close and then the running footsteps of his granddaughter. Hilly came bursting into the room, gave him a kiss and a hug, then bounded upstairs to watch her current favourite soap.

Anne threw down her bag on the big pine kitchen table. 'Anything I can do?' She was eyeing the kitchen with her usual alarm. This, she often thought, was how the Huns or the Visigoths would have gone about preparing a meal.

'Thank you, you can get me a drink.'

She poured him a whisky and soda and a glass of wine for herself.

'What are we having?'

'Wait and see.'

'How exciting.'

He ignored the irony and took a decent swig of his whisky. 'Well, what happened to the accused?'

'It was paracetamol,' she said. 'It's often that or overdoses of valium.'

'Where did he get it? I thought he was supposed

to be safe in your hospital?'

'That's the governor's line.'

'Don't you have security there?'

'Of course we do.'

'It doesn't sound all that good to me.'

'He's in secure accommodation now.'

They had taken him from Kingstown hospital to one of the category A rooms in the prison hospital. When she had first come they were still building these. They had bars placed outside the windows, no radiators along the walls or window catches on which, like Jameson, a prisoner could anchor shoe laces, a piece of towelling, or the arm of a shirt and strangle himself.

She had gone to see Mason before picking up Hilly from a friend's house. He was white-faced and wan.

'How do you feel now?' she had asked.

'Sick.'

'We'll have to check your blood regularly now because of the paracetamol.'

'Liver damage? They told me at the hospital. As if it'd bother me. Only finish the job. Why didn't you just leave me?'

'Can't do that.'

He looked around the room. His mattress was its only piece of furniture.

'The other room had lavatories,' he said.

'These don't.'

'In case I try to drown myself?'

She shook her head. 'We sometimes need to check fluid intake and lavatories have water in them.'

'Why bother?'

'Suicide risks.'

'Suicide in prison isn't very popular is it? I mean if the press get hold of it.'

'Not very.'

'What about life imprisonment for something you didn't do. Is that popular?'

What could she say?

'What *did* you say?' her father asked.

'I thought of something Tom Melville had mentioned and I asked him if he had ever tried to kill himself before.'

'And?'

'And he said: "What do you think?" It was meant to sound as though the very question was ridiculous and yet it didn't. It seemed as though he was really asking a question for which he wanted an answer.'

'You're losing me.'

'Asking whether in my opinion he was the kind of man who would have tried in the past.'

'That's all speculation. You're too sensitive. But I suppose that's inevitable after the what'shisname business.'

'Jameson. And don't think he hasn't been in all our minds.'

'Your trouble is that you don't really want to find out that Chitty has tried before. It'd detract from your belief in his innocence.'

29

'Yes, it would.'

He turned to the saucepan. 'Those eggs should be hard-boiled by now shouldn't they?'

'How long have they been boiling?'

'About half an hour.'

'The thirty-minute egg. That's a new one. They'll be like rocks.' She looked at her watch. 'The programme's finished.'

There was the sound of Hilly's feet on the stairs and she came into the room. 'You *never* look at the answering machine!' she said.

'Is there a message?'

'Grandpa never looks either!'

'It's your machine,' Henry said. 'Supper time.'

Anne went up to her bedroom and switched on the machine. There was a sound of static that seemed to come from a distant planet and then a voice said, 'It is I, Watchman Malopo, I am eh-speakin' to you from Johannes-beg, I am eh-speakin' on a public telephone and I have little money.'

It was a voice that Anne knew well from her childhood. A loved one. The voice of someone who had not only acted as a kind of mother to her – complementing Henry's paternal role – but was also a Baloo to her Mowgli.

She wanted to greet him. To tell him how much she missed him. To ask why he was in Johannesburg, so far from his home in Lesotho.

The machine went on remorselessly. He must

have moved slightly away from the mouthpiece of the telephone because she could only hear a jumble of phrases and thought they had to do with his sister. But there were the words 'school' and 'university' and they didn't make much sense.

Then, as though in answer to her unspoken question, she heard him say ' . . . airport and I am waiting for the plane. I am coming Thursday. I cannot speak more because the money is running out.'

The machine cut off at this point and Anne heard it rewind. She stood as though in a dream and then went slowly downstairs.

Hilly was picking at a mess of mashed hard-boiled eggs and tomato ketchup which even Henry did not feel matched the description of 'huevos a la flamenca' from his little book.

'Leave it if you don't want it,' Anne said.

Henry opened his mouth, then closed it.

Hilly helped herself to a plate of ice-cream instead and went up to bath.

'You'd better have another drink,' Anne said to her father. 'I know I'm going to.'

But as she told him what Watch was about to do he seemed to become more cheerful rather than more worried.

'What are we going to do with him?' she said. 'He can't stay here.'

'Why not?'

'Well, where?'

'I've got a spare bedroom. He can sleep there.'

'But . . . I mean we live differently and—'

'Not very differently from when I was retired. He lived with me then. We got on perfectly well. Don't forget I know Watch even better than I know you or Hilly. My God, I had him for nearly forty years.'

'But what's he going to *do*?' She projected herself into a future where she had to worry not only about Hilly and her father but also about an elderly man from Lesotho who could do many things like seeing that her father's legal wig and gown were perfect every morning, like keeping an accurate diary of where and when he was to appear on the bench, like organising a staff of women to cook and wash and clean, like driving Henry's car, and who could, when he wanted to, cook amazing meals on dried cow dung, but who had no experience of life in an English cathedral city.

'He's going to do what he's always done,' Henry said. 'He's going to look after us. He looked after me for most of my life and he looked after you when you were little and he'd have looked after your mother if she'd let him. And there's no use you saying things have changed and black people no longer look after white people because it doesn't matter whether they're white, black or brindle, some people look after other people because that's what they do in life and Watch is one of them. And in turn we shall look after him. Good Lord, he's sixty-six if he's a day and we're his family.'

'He had a family in Maseru.'

'And they took him for every penny he had. Don't you remember how unhappy he was when he called us from the Holiday Inn in Maseru?'

'What I remember is that when we called him back they had to get him out of the gaming rooms.'

'All right, maybe he was gambling. But he told me he was also paying for the education of a niece or nephew – or both.'

She remembered the words 'school' and 'university' from the message on the machine.

'Anyway I told him he could,' Henry said. 'And you wouldn't want me to go back on my word, would you?'

'Told him he could what?'

'Come over and stay for a while if he needed to.'

A thought came into her head. 'You've been planning this, haven't you?'

'What?'

'Bringing Watch over.'

'Nonsense.'

'Yes you have, I can sense when you're lying. Well, he's your problem.'

'Why should he be a problem?'

'Just think how lonely he's going to be. How strange.'

'You do talk rubbish. He'll be with his people. You can't want more than that.'

* * *

33

The torch was a powerful one and it lit up the hedgerows and the path Lily was walking. She was glad of the torch's power, it gave her a feeling of security. Barry had told her that the American police used torches like it. He wanted her to have something that gave a brilliant light and was heavy enough to be a weapon. He'd always been afraid of leaving her by herself, but like most Navy wives she had got used to being alone.

She walked up the path towards the hill. The village was beneath and behind her. The wide path was called a 'gallop' but no one rode along it now because it ended after a few hundred yards in a five-bar gate on which were the signs: 'Private Property. Keep Out'.

Lily could remember when this was all open. She and Sandra had walked it many times. So had most of the others in the village. It was where they took their dogs. In those days it had been owned by Mrs Drayton, then she had sold a large part of it to the Chittys and that had been the end of the 'gallops'. They'd been replaced by gates, barbed-wire fences, notices.

She came to the gate. The night sky glowed ahead of her where Kingstown lay, but nearer was the glow from the Chittys' house.

'Where?' Lily said softly to Sandra. 'You must tell me where.'

Sandra's voice hadn't come again after that one terrible phrase, but Lily knew she was near. If only they could make more contact: if only Sandra would converse, tell her things, answer questions.

Sandra said nothing and Lily paused at the gate. 'Here?' she whispered.

But the police had been here as they'd been everywhere on the Chittys' land. They'd brought sniffer dogs and heat-seeking equipment and they'd even brought the latest archaeological scanners. They hadn't found Sandra.

'But I will,' Lily said, and even as she said it her heart failed her. It was so dark and there was so much land to search: fields of winter wheat and barley, grazing, coppices and woodland.

Would she go by day? Would they let her? Or would it have to be in the dark, by the light of Barry's torch?

She tried the gate but it was held by a chain and padlock. She was wearing trousers and she clambered over. It took her a moment or two but she reached the ground on the other side in one piece.

What was she to look for? Disturbed ground? But after all these months the grass would have grown and the earth would have become solid.

The house was about two hundred yards ahead of her on the top of the slope. It was a raw pile that had started off in the last century as a workman's cottage and had been extended several times. Ridge Cottage it had been called then, now it was called Ridge Farm.

35

Well, she wasn't going up to the farm. To her left the land fell away into the river valley. There were paths there amidst the brambles and the wild willows. Was that where Sandra had been hidden? Had she been buried by the river?

The torchlight played on a path and she took it. 'Here?' she whispered. 'Tell me, dearest.'

And then she saw another light bobbing, bobbing, like a firefly. It came nearer and she stopped.

'What the hell do you want?' a man's voice said. He shone the torch in her face. She gripped hers as Barry had told her to, like a weapon.

'Oh, it's you, Lily,' he said. 'What d'you want?'

'To find her,' Lily said.

Samuel Chitty was smoking a roll-up. He drew on it and threw it down.

'The police have looked,' he said.

'She's here,' Lily said.

'You'd best go, Lily.'

'I won't. Not till I find her.'

He gripped her arm. 'Go home, Lily.'

He walked with her up the path towards the gate. He had keys on him and in a moment the lock was open and she was through. He turned away and went up the hill to his home.

She watched him, unaware of the figure that floated up through the grass behind her.

She turned. A white face shrouded in a cloak seemed to hover in the darkness.

'Oh, my God!'

'Is it you, Lily?'

Mrs Drayton took her arm. Her hand was cold. 'What are you doing?'

'Looking for Sandra.' She began to cry again.

Then Mrs Drayton did an uncharacteristic thing: she put her arm around her and said, 'We haven't been very kind to you have we, Lily?'

5

'That's a funny name,' Hilly said.

'Watch? No funnier than Hilary.'

'Yes, it is.'

She was in the bath and Anne was standing in the doorway. She had changed out of her day clothes and was wearing a light-cream sweat-shirt and jeans. She took a brush from the cabinet and began to brush her short, dark hair.

'Tick tick . . . I'll call him Clock.' Hilly squeezed the soap until it leapt from her hand onto the floor.

Anne gave it back to her without comment; she had planned this conversation and did not want it sidetracked.

'His real name's Watchman. That's what his father was, a watchman, so he named his son after his job.'

'It sounds silly.'

Anne watched Hilly. All her actions and reactions were pointing to her unease and it was not difficult to understand. They had lived together in London, just the two of them. Then they had moved to Kingstown with Henry and there had been three of them. Hilly had now got used to her grandfather being in the same house, indeed they had become great friends, but in the beginning things had been difficult. Now someone else was going to arrive.

'Why do we have to have him?' Hilly said.

'I told you. He's coming for a holiday to see Grandpa and me – and you of course.'

'And then he'll go back to this place . . .'

'Lesotho. It's a country in the southern part of Africa. It's only a small country but the people are nice and it's got the most lovely mountains. I lived there when I was your age.'

'With Grandpa?'

'And Watch. He looked after both of us.'

'Is there a Mrs Watch?'

'No, darling, he never married. He wasn't the marrying kind and I think he was too busy with Grandpa.'

'If he wasn't married then he hasn't got any children.'

Anne decided not to go into the complex possibilities of this and simply said, 'No.'

'Well, he won't know how to treat me then.'

'Why not? He knew how to treat me.'

'You're different. You grew up in Africa.'

'Darling, you're making a terrible fuss about nothing. You're going to like him a lot, I just know that.' But Hilly's face registered grave doubt. The phone rang and Anne answered it in her bedroom.

'Dr Vernon?'

'Speaking.'

'This is Sophie Lennox.'

'Who?'

'I was the researcher for the television programme we did on Mr Jameson.'

Anne felt cold fingers touch her heart. 'Oh, yes, I remember now.'

'That was for *Justice Today*.'

'Yes.'

'I've actually moved since then. I'm working for a different production company. We're doing a series on the British penal system and one of the aspects we're hoping to look at is the possibility . . . or let me put it another way, what happens to members of the prison service – and prisoners for that matter – when a prisoner is thought by them to be innocent.'

'You've done Harold Jameson. That's the only case I have any knowledge of.'

'I was thinking about this man Chitty. I was wondering if what happened in court today had anything to do with—'

'To do with what?'

'Well . . . you know, whether there was something sinister about his collapse in the dock.'

Before she could stop herself, Anne said: 'Absolutely not.'

'Do you know what made him collapse then?

'Stress. Worry. Depression. Take your pick. It often happens but usually in prison so it's not quite so public. We've got him in our hospital and he's being well looked after.'

'Wasn't he taken to Kingstown General after he collapsed?'

'Yes, he was.'

'Why didn't you just take him back to your own prison hospital?'

'Because Kingstown General is nearer the courts and it might have been something more serious.'

'A heart attack?'

'Anything.'

'So it definitely wasn't a suicide attempt?'

'That's right.'

'Okay, thanks, Dr Vernon.'

Anne put down the phone and saw that her hand was shaking.

'Mummy, the soap's on the floor again,' Hilly shouted.

Later, when her daughter was in bed and asleep, Anne dialled Tom's home number.

The phone rang and rang and she could see it clearly in her mind's eye in the big old wooden house where he lived by himself.

'Come on!' she said aloud.

But it wasn't answered.

'Coffee? You don't want coffee. You want something stronger than that.' Elizabeth Drayton poured a stiff whisky, added a little water and gave it to Lily.

'Thank you.'

To Lily, who hardly drank anything these days, the whisky tasted very strong. She'd had a glass or two when Barry was at home, but when he went to sea she'd always stopped, she had seen too many naval wives hitting the bottle out of loneliness.

'Well, Lily . . .'

It was said as though it was a colophon placed at the end of a short scene: as though something had ended. But it wasn't that way at all, for Elizabeth Drayton picked up where she had left off at the gate.

'It's not as though we're not sympathetic. You mustn't feel that.'

The whisky seemed to go quickly to Lily's head and she decided not to answer. She looked about her instead. They were in a small sitting-room. She had been to the house several times for charity events but they had been held in the big drawing-room. This was more intimate. The old leather chesterfield and the two leather armchairs were worn and in some places torn. A log was smouldering in the grate even though it was a warm spring evening, for the house was cold and she noticed that the central heating system was of the massive pre-war variety, bound in parts by waterproof tape in an effort to stop the rusted joints leaking onto the carpets. On the walls were paintings of animals: stags, horses, partridges and dogs. Elizabeth Drayton no longer looked like some floating ghost as she had earlier. Her face, which must once have been beautiful, was lined by decades of wind and harsh weather.

'We haven't ever really had a chat, have we Lily?'

'A chat?'

'You know what I mean. A good talk.'

As far as Lily was concerned their conversation had always been totally artificial and contrived. She'd first come with Barry to a charity fête in the house not long after they'd arrived in Stepton, and she had sometimes greeted Mrs Drayton in the village shop, but she'd hardly seen her for the past few years. Since her son's death she had become something of a recluse. Then she had started selling her land.

'I know what you're thinking, Lily, you're thinking, what does this woman want to talk about?'

'No, I wasn't, I—'

'Yes, you were. Well, there are all sorts of things we can talk about, the village and how it's treated you all these years, but we'll get to that.'

She waved the whisky bottle.

'No thank you, I'm not used to it.'

'It's a great comfort. Specially when you've lost someone dear.'

Lily had never seen her like this. With her long, dark cloak and her white hair and her lined face she reminded Lily of a book of Victorian paintings which had been in her house when she was a child. The women in those paintings had worn long cloaks and had very white faces and huge eyes but they'd been younger than Mrs Drayton.

'We're two of a kind, Lily. I suppose you realise that.'

'I'm not sure I understand, Mrs Drayton.'

'I call you Lily and you call me Mrs Drayton. I suppose that sums up the English village attitude, doesn't it? I want to change that if I can, at least as far as you're concerned. What I mean by two of a kind is that I lost Rollo and you've lost Sandra and we haven't anyone else. No other children. No husband. Understand? So I want you to call me Elizabeth. Do you think you can do that? Try. Say Elizabeth.'

'Elizabeth.'

'You see? Right. Now, Lily I want to help you find Sandra. That's what you want, isn't it? I know that's what I would want. When I heard Rollo was dead that's all I wanted. I made a bargain with God. I said let me recover his body and I'll never do another thing wrong. Never. But God doesn't work like that. I mean, how could I find Rollo? How could anyone find him in that howling desert? So I had to live with it, but at least I knew he was dead and I knew whereabouts his body was. You don't, do you?'

'No.'

'And we want to mourn, don't we?'

'How can we if we don't know whether our baby is dead or not?'

'But we do know.'

'How do you mean?'

'I was in court too. The police forensic scientists

have matched the blood on Mason's watch strap and . . .'

'But that doesn't mean she's dead!'

'Lily, this is what I went through. The Ministry of Defence couldn't say for certain about Rollo. They knew his plane had been hit by an Iraqi missile but they didn't know if he had ejected or not. And I said to myself: Of course he did and the Ministry will call from London and tell me he's fine. But they didn't call, not with good news anyway. His body was never found.'

Lily said, 'That's why . . . I mean, I would've looked . . . but I said to myself she'll be back. I used to stand at the windows and look down the lane, or listen for her footsteps. I listened and listened . . . all night sometimes.'

'I know that feeling.' Elizabeth's fingers began to fret at a piece of loose thread on the chesterfield. 'Have another.'

'Oh no, no more.'

'Come on, for God's sake. You cried at the gate. Cry again and let some of this out. The best way to make yourself cry is to get a little drunk.'

'But what would she say?'

'Who? Sandra? What d'you mean, what would she say?'

'She spoke to me.'

'When?'

'This evening. That's why I went out. She said, "Find me!" '

'Sandra told you to find her? But did she tell you *where* to find her? Lily, the police have been over and over the Chitty land.'

'I know.' And then she said desperately, 'When she spoke like that, I thought she *must* be dead.'

'Was that the first time you really thought she was dead?'

'Well, it isn't as easy as that, Mrs Drayton.'

'Elizabeth.'

'Elizabeth. It isn't as easy as that. Sometimes in a single day I can think: she's dead . . . she's not . . . yes, she is . . . no she's not . . . I want it to be over.'

'And it will be over.'

'I want to find her.'

'Yes, so that you can mourn.'

'It's the not knowing.'

'Of course it is.'

Lily sipped her second whisky. She said, 'People go mad.'

'What people?'

'People who lose their children and can't ever find them again. There's the mother of that little boy in Scotland . . .'

'Remind me.'

'The three or four little children tortured and murdered by those two people. And buried in a glen near Inverness.'

'Oh, yes, the Glen Murders, they called it. That was a long time ago. And they've found the bodies, haven't they?'

'Except for one, and the mother's gone mad, they say, and the psychiatrists say it's because the little boy hasn't been found.'

'That's what I'm telling you, Lily. People need to mourn. They need to be able to say: it's over.'

'I talk to her, you know. I talk to her every day.'

'I used to do that with Rollo after he was killed. Just little things. Nothing really important.'

'I tell her lots of things I never said. How much I loved her and what a wonderful girl she was. You never knew her much. But she was, you know. She was the sweetest and the most generous and the most gentle girl . . . And all for nothing!'

The tears came now.

'Let them out.' Elizabeth Drayton handed her a tissue. 'Let all the ache wash out.'

'I don't want to hear voices,' Lily said.

'And you won't. I'm going to do for you what they couldn't do for Rollo.'

'I don't want to go mad.' Lily said.

6

Kingstown Prison, apart from the cathedral, was the largest building in the town, larger even than the ruins of the medieval castle which brought so many tourists in summer. It had been built in the middle of the previous century in the then functional style of four wings designed as a cross, with an atrium in the middle. For a hundred years or more it had dominated the skyline, adding a note of Victorian gravity to the lighter proceedings down in the streets. Then the city council had decided that the gravity had become ponderous and that cypress trees were more cheerful, so they had planted a screen. Kingstown had begun to feel ashamed of its prison.

Anne parked her car in the small staff area and walked towards the huge wooden doors. Often she was reminded of her first view of them less than a year before, and the injunction from the officer in charge of the parking area to knock for admission.

Knock?

She had knocked and had entered a world entirely new to her, one she was still not sure about. Sometimes she saw her job as a challenge, sometimes the whole place seemed too much for her and she wanted out.

Knock?

Yes, she'd knocked. And so, a few moments later, had an old woman whose name she could no longer recall.

Bang. Bang. Bang.

That had been the beginning for Anne of the Billy Sweete case and the terrifying nightmare that had followed.*

Today she entered the prison with easy familiarity. Modern prison gatehouses have separate entrances for vehicles and pedestrians, but not Kingstown. It was still waiting for promised government money so the gatehouse was filled with deliveries: sides of bacon and boxes of cereals and pallets of bricks. Anne had to pick her way towards the gatekeeper's bullet-proof window and sidestep probation workers and girls from the administration offices who were either coming off duty or going on and flinging their tallies and keys into the wall funnel or picking others out of it. It was a noisy, dusty place and might have been part of a railway station in the days of steam, except for the officers with Alsatian dogs and the cuffed prisoners going off to court.

'Morning, doc,' the reception officer called as he dropped her keys into the collection tube. She lifted

* *Burn Out* by Alan Scholefield, Headline

them out and clipped them to the thin chain she wore on the belt of her trousers, then made her way across the yard to her room in the hospital. When she had first carried keys she had been aware of them all the time. She usually carried four, two pass keys for the internal prison gates, one for the hospital and one for doors and filing cabinets that only senior officers opened: what Tom called the secret service keys.

'Morning, doc,' a plump and friendly face said. This was Les Foley, who had come into the prison service as a warder and had later chosen to switch to the health-care staff. When she had first arrived, Tom had tried to make the clutter of staff titles and initials easier for her by telling her that Foley was the equivalent of a corporal in the Army. He was plump and dimpled and had had his hair lightened and she had always got on well with him.

'Is Dr Melville in yet?' she said.

'He's on the phone.'

'I'll go and see Mason Chitty. Have you taken blood?'

'Jeffrey said I wasn't to.'

'Why on earth not?'

He looked over his shoulder, came in and closed the door. There was something intimate about it, almost feminine. 'He's a bit put out by something.'

'Oh, dear.'

Jeffrey Jenks was the senior health-care officer

– the sergeant major of the hospital staff – and Anne had not formed the same friendly relationship with him as she had with Les Foley. 'What's brought this on?'

'It's something that started yesterday. Something Dr Melville said.'

'Do you know what it was?'

'Something about paracetamol.'

'Okay, thanks Les, I'll see what's what.'

She went to Jenks's cubby-hole in one of the corridors of the hospital. As usual he was working on his staff detail forms and as usual he pretended to be so busy that he could not look up. This was a behaviour pattern she had endured since she had joined the staff. She had the usual problems with some prisoners, the foul language, the sexual offers, the broad humour, but she had come to expect that and could handle it. It largely came from remand prisoners. Most of the sentenced men seemed to calm down once they knew what was happening to them. Jenks was the only member of staff with whom she had problems. Her father, who had met him once, described him as a 'typical bloody warrant officer, prickly as a porcupine'.

She looked at him now in his black trousers and dark-blue regulation jersey with the two pips on his shoulder tabs. His black shoes gleamed and his trousers were ironed within an inch of their lives.

'Mr Jenks, have you a moment?'

He seemed to think about this. His finger held

52

his place, then he turned his thin face towards her.

'Have you taken Mason Chitty's blood?'

He had been expecting the question, she knew that, and she could see the anger in his face by the way he worked his jaw.

'No, I haven't.'

'I thought I asked you to. Or at least to get someone to do it. Can you tell me what this is all about?'

He leaned back in his chair. 'You know what it's all about. Dr Melville accused me of being irresponsible with the paracetamol. If that is so, then I'm too irresponsible to take blood.'

His voice had risen and she did not want the whole of the hospital to be privy to what looked like becoming a first-rate row.

'Will you come into my room please, Mr Jenks.'

'I'm sorry, but I've got a great deal of work to—'

'Will you come into my room, please.'

He nodded, more to himself than to Anne, as though to be sure of his side of the argument, and seemed to decide he could not refuse someone who was a much higher grade than himself. He rose and followed her into her room. She decided not to sit down in case he stood, but leaned against the examination couch.

'May I remind you that Mason Chitty is my patient and has been since he came.'

'I am not going to be spoken to like some kind of servant,' Jenks said.

'I'm sorry if you think I'm speaking to you like that.'

'I didn't mean you. Dr Melville spoke very rudely to me last evening.'

'Can you tell me what he said?'

'Why not? You may as well hear it from me before there's a POA meeting.'

'Why drag the union into this?'

'You don't think I'm going to stand for that sort of accusation, do you? Why do you think we join the Prison Officers' Association?'

'Please Mr Jenks, you're leaving me far behind.'

'Very well.' His lips came together in the pedantic line she knew so well. 'I just want to know exactly what the medical staff want us to do!'

She started to speak but he went on, 'One minute we're told that prisoners are human beings and must control their own lives and we mustn't stand over them while they take their medicines and sometimes not even when they take something stronger. So when Chitty says he's got a headache, as he said the past few days, we, the health-care staff aren't supposed to come running to the doctors to ask if we can give paracetamol – or are we?'

'Of course not.'

'Well, Dr Melville said we should, and that means we don't have our own responsibility, that we're not trusted. And if we're not trusted to give bathroom-cupboard drugs like paracetamol then we can't be trusted to take blood, can we?'

'I think you're exaggerating.'

'Exaggerating! On the one hand we've got the doctors wanting to stay on schedule and on the other we've got prisoners banging on the hatch all day long wanting their methadone or their valium or something. I mean it's not right. We're at the sharp end and we're the ones who suffer stress and depression, not the doctors. Now you say you don't trust us!'

'That's not true. Dr Melville and I trust you implicitly. Goodness, without you the place would fall apart!'

In his eyes she could see the anger recede.

'It *would* fall apart,' he said. 'That's for sure.'

She soothed him as much as she could and then went into the room where Chitty was held.

"Morning, Mason,' she said.

He was lying on his side with his knees curled up against his stomach and did not look at her.

'Oh dear,' she said, 'not you too. I've just had the silent treatment from someone else.'

Unlike the reaction from Jenks who, she knew, had been boiling inside, she had never been certain with Mason. He seemed, like an animal, to go doggo, to become cut off from his surroundings and reality. Sometimes she would find him crying quietly. Sometimes he would seem to be catatonic. That had not been the case early on. Soon after his arrest he had been frightened and angry by turns. He had protested his innocence with a vehemence she had rarely witnessed, and it was this that had troubled her, especially after the Jameson episode.

In a way the two cases were similar. They were both violent crimes. Jameson had been arrested, tried and sentenced to life imprisonment for the murder of a young boy of nine. It had been a gruesome killing: rape, strangulation, the dumping of the body in a pond – the kind of killing the tabloids fed on like great white sharks.

There had been tremendous pressure to convict someone. Although Jameson had protested his innocence over and over again, and although the evidence was not very strong, he had been convicted and sentenced. Then he'd killed himself. Two weeks later a witness had changed his story and the boy's uncle had been arrested.

By that time it was too late for Jameson.

But not too late for a second media feeding frenzy. And now entered the heavyweight TV documentary companies because a number of IRA 'terrorists' had also been released and wrongful imprisonment was flavour of the month.

She looked at Mason and could have been looking at Jameson. This was how he had begun to react when the stress produced depression. And like Jameson, Mason's state of distress had caused her to hospitalise him for several weeks before the trial.

Gradually she had become more and more convinced that he too might be innocent, especially as no body had ever been found. The DNA evidence was damning but the bloodstains just might have been caused the way he said they had.

She fetched a vacutainer and said, 'Where would you like it, Mason?'

He did not respond, nor had she expected him to. She drew blood from his inner arm, broke off the needle and dropped it into the sharpsafe, took sharpsafe and full vacutainer to her office and filled in a form for the lab in Kingstown General.

When she went back to his room Chitty had not moved. 'See you later,' she said. Then she locked the door. She wanted to see Tom, *had* to see him after what had happened the previous evening, but when she looked at her watch she realised he would already be at surgery in the main block.

It was beginning to look like this wasn't her day.

Sandra ... Sandra ... Are you there, love?

Lily is in her bedroom holding a pair of Sandra's gloves as though to bring her nearer. She holds them tightly, hoping Sandra will talk to her once more; will answer questions.

Had Sandra really spoken?

Was this what the woman in Scotland had experienced? Was this what had driven her mad?

You didn't have to go mad.

Mrs Drayton ... Elizabeth ... had lost Rollo, shot down in the Gulf War. Lily remembers when his name was added to the war memorial in the village under the names of those who had died in the Great War and the Second World War.

She remembers when his name was unveiled. Rollo Nigel Drayton. Twenty-eight years old. Older than Sandra by quite a few years.

Elizabeth had been at the unveiling and she hadn't wept and certainly hadn't gone mad.

Sandra, love, I'm going to find you and I'm going to bury you properly and mourn you properly. And I'm going to be helped – but you know that, don't you?

Do you know everything? About how I met Elizabeth and what she said?

Maybe you don't. Maybe I should tell you. And I will. I'll tell you everything, so you'll know.

We're having our first search meeting tomorrow up at the big house and I've been asked to make scones and a cake. I never made scones after your father died because you never liked them. But that's what she wants. Scones and a cake. So I'll make a fruit cake. You used to eat that sometimes.

Oh, Sandra, we'll search and search until we find you, my love . . .

She begins to cry again. Finally she fights the tears and stops them.

She is looking into the darkness of the window above Sandra's bed and thinks for a moment she sees her face.

She feels cold and desperate. I don't want to go mad, she says aloud.

Will I?

But Sandra doesn't answer.

7

'No, this is mine,' Anne said.

'Don't be ridiculous,' Tom said. 'I never get invited out by attractive women and I'd like to contribute. Anyway, I'm your boss and what I say goes. So, what'll you have?'

They were in the King's Arms in a small, cobbled street away from the main thoroughfares. It was a pub they had made their own. In winter it had a glowing coal fire and in summer a small terrace at the back with tables under a huge, shady plane tree. Its big advantage was that none of the prison staff used it.

She smiled. 'You'll regret your generosity when you hear what I've got to say.'

'Oh dear, let's have a drink first.'

'I'll have a spritzer.'

He ordered two white-wine spritzers and carried them out to the terrace where they had the shade to themselves.

'Here's to absent friends,' he said, 'like Jeffrey bloody Jenks.'

'I caught him in a very bad mood,' she said.

'I know, Les Foley told me. He said he listened at your door.'

'I'll remember that. I think I calmed Jenks down. He was talking about a POA meeting and it all began to sound a bit rough.'

'I didn't accuse him of anything, you know. All I said was he should have talked more to Chitty before handing out the paracetamol. He might have seen what state he was in.'

'I should probably have told him not to hand it out in the first place or at least to let me know he was. He's calmed down now. I must say I wouldn't like to be Mrs Jeffrey Jenks. There is one, I suppose.'

'Chris.'

'He never mentions her.'

'He's never brought her to any social functions.'

'Anyway, that isn't what I wanted to talk to you about. It's rather more serious than injuries to Jenks's pride.'

He waited.

'Something happened last night that scared me.' She told him about the telephone call from the TV researcher and what she had said in reply.

'Let me get this straight,' he said. 'She asked you if Chitty had taken something in the dock?'

'Not quite in those words and not necessarily in the dock, but the sense of it was there: had Mason tried to kill himself because he was innocent?'

'And you said no, that what had happened was he'd collapsed because of—'

'Stress, depression . . . the usual . . . In other words I lied.'

He nodded. 'Yes, I can see that.'

'God, I'm sorry. I just didn't think. The call came at night and to the house and—'

'Of course you weren't ready for it. Who would have been? I'd probably have done the same. It's called a white lie. You were trying to protect the prison staff as well as Chitty.'

'But it doesn't alter the fact that it was a lie and that the person I was most protecting was myself since Mason is my patient. And if this girl finds out it was a lie . . .'

'It's not the first time TV has been lied to and it won't be the last.'

'It still doesn't help the present case. What if she does find out? What happens then?'

'If she was a print journalist we might be in trouble, but with TV . . . she said it was a documentary, didn't she?'

'Part of a series on the prison service.'

'I wish they'd think of something else to pin their series on – like an investigation into the quality of TV programmes. If she'd been a newspaper reporter she'd already have found out about his stomach being pumped. The nick's been at the centre of both forms of press interest before and I'll take TV over the tabloids for a quieter life.'

She began to relax. 'You're giving me confidence.'

'Look, you've got your plate full with Chitty, let me take this over. I'll have a word with the governor because he's got to know and I'll also find out more about this projected series of programmes from Holroyd at the Home Office. He's our press officer so he should be able to find out about a series like that – and about the girl, for that matter. Have another.'

She shook her head. 'I'd go to sleep this afternoon.' She stood up. 'I really am very grateful.'

He rose with her. 'I'm going to see my mother this weekend, why don't you come along? You haven't got the duty.'

'I want to take Hilly out, but thanks.'

'I meant bring her too. She'd love the river and she can play with Beanie. It doesn't take all that long to get there.'

There was a sudden tension between them. It came and went as though controlled by a thermostat.

Until recently she had been having an affair with a wealthy businessman and there had been talk of marriage, mainly by him and his mother. But she had put an end to it and paid him back money she had borrowed to buy the house. For some time she had felt a wonderful sense of freedom. But that had gradually and naturally faded as the question came to the front of her mind: What now?

She had learned a great deal about herself since Hilly's father died. He was the only man she had ever really loved but what she had learned was that she hated being alone and she liked the company of men. She knew this was unfashionable in some feminist groups but she couldn't help that. She was the only woman doctor in a world of men and also knew that this, or something like it, was the subject of a thousand cheap novels. It didn't change her feelings though.

What made this invitation problematical was that it came from Tom, and Tom was not an ordinary man. He was attractive, that was undeniable, but he was also her boss.

'Can I see how things pan out?' she said. 'I've got a complication.'

'Oh?'

'An old member of my father's staff in Africa is coming to stay.'

'Not the one with the odd name. Something to do with time?'

'Watch. Yes, he's coming over for . . . well, for a holiday I suppose.'

'No problem. You let me know and in the meantime, I'll start the—'

'The rehabilitation of Anne Vernon.'

He laughed. 'I wouldn't put it like that.'

Ping . . . pong. Ping . . . pong . . . went the message gong at Heathrow Airport. Then came the voice of the female information officer:

'Will Mr Watchman Malopo, a passenger on flight three-two-one from Johannesburg please come to the information desk. That's Mr Watchman

Malopo who arrived on the Johannesburg flight.
Would he please come to the information desk.'

Henry Vernon stood at the desk.

'You sure he was on the flight?' he said to the
information officer.

'Yes, I'm sure.'

'Well, I've been waiting for God knows how long
and—'

'I told you sir, the flight was late, And—'

'Good mornin', Judge.'

Henry swung round and there, like some dark-
skinned ghost, stood the man who had looked after
him for nearly forty years. He felt a surge of
something quite unfamiliar rise up inside him and
then, hastily and more abrasively than he had
meant, said, 'You're late, Watch.'

'The plane was late, Judge.'

He was older and thinner than Henry
remembered, but the prim expression which he did
remember was still there. Lesotho is a country of
mountains and it produces mountain people. Watch
was one such; stringy, tensile, gaunt and bony, he
was dressed in something Henry had never thought
to see him wear, a purple-and-gold tracksuit. There
was not an ounce of fat on him and his face bore an
expression of martyrdom, which, in the past, had
been noted on the faces of others who had had
prolonged dealings with Henry.

'Well, it's good to see you, Watch.'

'And good to see you too, Judge.'

'Let's find your luggage and get the hell out of here.' Watch held up a small case. 'Is that all? Where are your clothes?'

'My sister wanted my suits and eh-jackets.'

'What for?'

'Her boys. They gave me this.' He touched the tracksuit.

'Oh Lord. We'll have to see about that.'

They went to the car-park and there they had their first row. Watch refused to get in.

'You not drivin', Judge.'

'Don't be bloody silly, of course I'm driving. You're not my servant any more, you're my friend. You don't have to work.'

But Watch stood by the side of the car in his purple-and-gold tracksuit clutching his small suitcase to his chest.

'I mean that, Watch,' Henry said. 'This is going to be a holiday for you. We're going to do the work, and we're going to look after you.'

Watch pressed his lips together and showed the whites of his eyes.

'I know what life must have been like for you,' Henry continued. 'All those kids of your sister's needing clothes and money. Well, it's different now. So hop in and we'll get going.'

'You not drivin',' Watch said.

'For God's sake, we can do without—'

'You a very bad driver, Judge.'

'What?'

65

'It is true. You drivin' your cars down mountains and into rivers.'

It was indeed true. In Africa, Henry had owned a series of specialist cars, with names like Lanchester and Jowett and Armstrong Siddeley, names no longer known, and not known at any time in remote African countries. He had driven them, as Watch said, down mountains. He had also driven them over cliffs, and into farm dams, and at least one had been abandoned in the Kalahari. Watch had finally taken over the driving – to the deep gratitude of several chiefs and headmen who had feared for their lives and for the lives of their people. The cars had also lasted longer.

Henry said, 'That's a bloody lie, Watch, and you might as well get used right at the beginning—'

'Watchman bin in the car with the Judge. He knows.'

Henry paused. When Watch slipped into the third person it was a sign of his agitation and Henry knew it of old. The next stage was that Watch would become querulous and wearisome, like some old woman, and then Henry would regret his arrival.

'All right then, what do you want to do?'

'I will drive. You will eh-tell me the way.'

Henry's car was a vast, elderly Rover which was heavy enough to flatten the average contemporary sedan without disturbing the Rover's back-seat passengers.

'Oh, Christ, have it your bloody way,' Henry said.

And that's how they came to Kingstown, with
Watch driving very slowly down the motorways,
and Henry giving him directions, some of which
were wrong.

8

'Thank you for coming, ladies and gentlemen. I don't have to tell you why we're here. You know all that well enough.'

Vice-Admiral Sir Peter Pattinson, RN (Retd), was seated at the writing table at the end of Elizabeth Drayton's large drawing-room. In front of him was a small group of villagers sitting neatly on the chairs provided.

The Admiral took off his wrist-watch and placed it face up on the table in front of him, then pulled a large writing-block towards him and unscrewed an expensive-looking fountain pen.

'It's a very sad occasion,' he said. 'Sad for us all. But we're going to do something about that. Can't change the facts but we can change the circumstances, at least for Lily Benson. As you know, we've come to talk about finding Sandra's body and for that we're going to need working parties.'

He wrote down the date and time of the meeting and then the words: *working parties.*

'Right. Let's see whom we've got and I'll write out an attendance sheet, then we can discuss objectives and planning. We have Mrs Drayton and

Lily, of course.' The pen scratched along the rough paper. 'And myself . . .' He wrote down his own name.

The Admiral was in his sixties and had come to Stepton with his wife a few years earlier. She had died and he continued to live there. He loved his garden and his golf and his pint of bitter at the Mayfly. In his day he had been a good golfer, single figures, but now spent much of his leisure with a fly-rod on the Step. He was of medium height, thin, with sparse grey hair. He had a lined and chiselled face, and light-blue eyes.

Lily watched him as he wrote down the names. She had never said much to the Admiral. He had come to the village after Barry had died. Perhaps it might have been different when Barry was still alive, but then again, it might not. An admiral and a lieutenant who had come up through the ranks did not strike her as having a great deal in common.

She wanted to look around her, but couldn't. At this moment, for the first time since her wedding day, she knew she was the centre of attention; she was the reason why all these people were here. Not that there were many. A dozen, perhaps, and some she knew better than others.

There was Betty Sugden who had been Sandra's best friend. From the time they had been teenagers they had been inseparable and early on Lily had been jealous of Betty's prettiness. But as they grew older Sandra had developed her own good looks and style.

Sitting behind her was a horse dealer named Mitchell. Even if she hadn't seen him when she came in she would have known it was him by the smell of stables – a mixture of dung, urine and straw – that was unmistakably his perfume.

Mitchell scared her somewhat. He was a man who kept to himself and his horses. She didn't know his first name. He was called Mitchell or Mitch by everyone. He was in his thirties, tall and dark with long, greasy hair. People said he was half gypsy. He supplied firewood and did fencing and traded horses and anything else he could lay his hands on.

Then there was Kenny. But he didn't count, really. He was middle-aged but acted as though he was seven or eight. He was always riding an invisible motorbike. Once he had ridden it into one of the big circulating doors of the supermarket in Kingstown and had smashed up the door and himself. Kenny came to every meeting in Stepton, every church service, wedding, christening and funeral, every fête and sports event – and as many private parties as he could get into.

He was that part of life the villagers put up with – though Sandra had not. She had told Lily more than once that he had tried to get his hand up her skirt. Lily had said, 'He's retarded, he doesn't know what he's doing. Don't worry about him.'

And Sandra had said, 'You'd worry about him if

he was trying to get inside your pants.'

Sometimes Lily had wished her daughter would not use phrases like that, now she told herself she was being silly, that her objection was a 'generation thing'. This was a phrase that Sandra had often used.

Kenny had been interviewed by the police when Sandra went missing. The village didn't believe he had anything to do with it but the police, looking for a suspect, had tried hard to prove that he had. He'd told them he had been out riding his motorbike when Sandra had disappeared and they had asked to see his bike. When they realised it was an invisible bike they would have carted him off to the cells if Elizabeth Drayton hadn't said she'd seen him on her land. No, Lily thought, you only had to look at Kenny to know he wouldn't have killed Sandra. She'd have known how to deal with him if he'd attempted to attack her. But Mason Chitty . . . she let the name come into her mind . . . he could have all right.

' . . . rang Chief Superintendent Bramell last night,' the Admiral was saying, and she concentrated again. 'I'm not sure he would have spoken to me if we hadn't fished together occasionally, but he did and it supports everything we've heard. The search was thorough. He said that with the modern infra-red equipment and also the scanner they borrowed it's pretty certain she was not buried on the Chitty's land. Of course, if Mason did it, as the police say he did, then he must know exactly where she is. But what we are here to talk about—'

There was a commotion near the doorway. A figure was coming through it dressed in a black-lycra costume of the kind that professional cyclists wear, and it fitted him like a second skin, showing, as Sandra had once said, 'everything that hangs between his legs'.

This was Mike Treagust. On his head was an orange cycling helmet and he was taking off a pair of cycling gloves. His face was dripping with sweat. He reminded Lily of the scene in Barry's favourite film, *The Graduate*, where the young Dustin Hoffman appears wearing his new diving gear.

'Sorry. The train was late,' Mike said. He always cycled home from the train.

'I didn't wait,' a woman said. 'I wasn't going to sit around waiting for you.'

This was Mike's wife, Magda. In her late twenties, she had a bush of black hair and a chiselled and rather thin white face. She was wearing a baby-carry over her shoulders and Lily wondered whether she intended to give the infant her breast.

'Sit down, Mike,' the Admiral said, and went on with his lecture about infra-red search machines and archaeological scanners. Then he began to form separate working parties and all the names had to be written down again. At this point Elizabeth

Drayton nudged Lily and they went off to make the tea. The kitchen was vast, the Aga cooker was on and the air was stifling.

'The scones look lovely, Lily.'

'Thank you.' Lily was pleased.

After tea the meeting broke up into what the Admiral called discussion groups. People became talkative, almost jovial. For the first time in months Lily felt less alone.

'I like his tracksuit, but I don't like him,' Hilly said. 'He's always looking at me.'

She and Anne were in Anne's bedroom and Hilly was putting on her pyjamas after her bath.

'Why shouldn't he look at you? You look at him.'

It had been a not very promising start to Watch's 'holiday'. That was how Anne thought of it, in inverted commas. He had hardly eaten anything at supper even though Henry had cooked smoked haddock and poached eggs.

'And he's always not talking,' Hilly said.

That was true. Watch had been silent for most of the meal. In fact he hadn't said much since she had come back that evening with Hilly.

There had been a strange meeting between Anne and Watch that was suffused with unspoken affection in the African way. She had had to remind herself that Basutos, like most mountain people, were not given to expressing emotions, and that women in Africa were still very much as they had

always been, second-class citizens. So she had
shaken Watch by the hand and said how nice it
was to see him and all the time she was seeing the
face of someone who had practically brought her
up. Without Watch to look after her, her childhood
would have been very different and she might not
have been able to live with her father after her
mother had bolted. He had always been travelling.
Sometimes the journeys between courtrooms were
hundreds of miles along bush tracks. He would not
have been able to keep an eye on her, but Watch
had been able and had done so. It was Watch who
had hired the black nannies to look after her, Watch
who had supervised her feeding, Watch who had
organised her life.

He had also organised, in each little town they
came to, the freedom of the local tennis club. Henry
at that time was a keen tennis player and had used
Anne as a tennis wall from the time she could hold
a racquet until she had gone overseas to study.

Watch had been the fixer in both their lives.

And now he was here in England and she was
happy to see him and worried about him at the
same time.

'Come on,' she said to her daughter, 'let's go and
see how Watch and Grandpa are getting on.'

'Grandpa doesn't like Watch.'

'Oh yes, he does.'

'He speaks to him like he doesn't.'

'Grandpa speaks like that to everybody. It's just

75

Grandpa.' Anne wondered how she could explain her father's use of brusqueness to hide his real emotions and decided it was too difficult.

'Let's go down,' she said.

'I want to watch TV.'

'Hilary!'

Hilly sighed deeply. 'Oh, all right.'

They had left Watch and Henry sitting round the kitchen table. Now only Henry was there.

'Gone to bed, I suppose,' he said to Anne's query.

'Was he all right?'

'I don't know. He didn't say anything, just got up and went to his room a few minutes after you'd taken Hilly up.'

'Oh dear, I hope nothing's wrong.'

'If Mr Watch has gone to bed can I go and watch TV?' Hilly said.

When she'd left Anne said. 'He's looking tired.'

'So would you be if you'd travelled from Basutoland.'

When Henry had first gone out to Africa it had been a different kind of world. He had travelled there by ocean liner. The lands to which he had travelled by train had been part of the British Empire and their stamps had borne the King's and then the Queen's heads. Zambia had been called Northern Rhodesia, Zimbabwe Southern Rhodesia, Tanzania had been called Tanganyika, and Lesotho had been Basutoland. Anne knew that often, when Henry was feeling upset about something African, he reacted in odd ways, one of which was simply to refuse to use the new names. Now he was worried about Watch, as she was herself.

He sat smoking his pipe, or at least sucking at it, which was about all he did, and reading the official journal of the Law Society.

'What are you going to do with him tomorrow?' Anne asked.

'Show him the law courts.'

'Will he like that?'

'Of course he will, he was my law clerk for long enough. And I'm going to buy him some new clothes. He can't go round Kingstown in a bloody tracksuit.'

'Hilly thinks it's lovely.'

He made a gurgling sound with his pipe.

'I'll go and say good-night to him,' she said.

'I wouldn't.'

Suddenly she was irritated. Her father was treating Watch as though they were still in Africa in the old days. Well, they weren't and she wasn't a child any longer. She was also a doctor and she wanted to make sure that Watch was all right, for he had looked more than tired.

So she ignored Henry and went down into the basement flat and knocked on Watch's door. He was sleeping in Henry's spare room, a small monastic area with a bed, table and light.

She got no reply and she called out, 'Watch, I've come to say good-night.'

Still no reply.

Was he asleep already?

She knocked again, more loudly. Still silence.

Worried that something might have happened to him she gently pushed open the door. The light was on and Watch was lying on the bed facing her, his eyes wide open.

'I wanted to see if you were comfortable and had everything you needed,' she said.

He remained silent. Oh God, she thought, not another Mason Chitty.

His face was gaunt and his thin body made to look thinner by the folds of the purple-and-gold tracksuit.

'Watch, it's lovely to have you here. Hilly thinks so too. She told me.'

Silence.

'I'll leave you now. I just thought I'd tell you about breakfast. We don't usually cook much nowadays, but you can have anything you like.'

This seemed to trigger a reaction. Watch turned away from her and faced the wall.

She realised how disorientated he must be. The flight, the strange house, the cathedral city with its narrow, crowded streets when he was used to the wide and empty roads of Maseru and Teyateyaneng. Add to that the fact that his former employer was waiting on him, and it wasn't difficult to understand his confusion.

'Good-night, Watch. Sleep well.'

*   *   *

Sandra . . . Sandra . . .

Lily has not put on the lights and Sandra's room is enveloped by dusk. She holds one of Sandra's woollen gloves and strokes it with tenderness.

We are going to find you, dearest.

This is usually the time that Lily cries, but now her eyes are dry.

We've had a meeting. It was chaired by Admiral Pattinson. We are going to form working parties. I'm with the Admiral and Betty and Mike Treagust and Mitchell, the horse dealer, and I think Kenny will come along too.

My love, we're going to look for you on Mrs . . . on Elizabeth Drayton's land because the police have been all over the Chittys' farm.

We're going to find you, sweetheart . . . Yes, we're going to find you . . .

9

'Can liver damage kill you?' Mason Chitty asked.

'Didn't they tell you that at the hospital?' Anne said.

'I suppose they did, I wasn't listening much at the time. That thing they stuffed down my throat wasn't very pleasant, you know.'

'No, but it drained the paracetamol out of your stomach.'

He was lying on his mattress on a raised concrete platform. It was a warm morning and the sun was hitting the suicide-proof windows.

She looked at his chart. 'Yes, liver damage can kill you. And we won't know you're really out of danger for a couple of weeks.'

'Is that how Jameson died? Liver damage?'

'I'd rather not talk about Jameson, Mason. Much rather talk about you and how you're getting on.'

He raised himself on his elbow and although he was only in his forties he was looking older due to loss of weight. His face was thin and she was reminded vividly of Watch the previous night.

'Tell me about liver damage, then,' he said.

'Not liver damage. *Your* liver damage. What the paracetamol has done. Maybe nothing, but it could have affected the liver's function, which is cleaning up the blood.'

'And?'

'Let's think positively.'

He lay back, put his arms under his head and said, 'Drinkers have liver damage and they go on for years.'

'That's different. That's the slow ruination of a liver. Yours was like a bomb hitting it.'

'Did Jameson drink, I wonder?'

'I don't know.'

'You never talk about him!'

'Mason, all I really have to discuss with you—'

'Is my medical condition. No answers to any questions you don't like.'

'That's my brief.'

'That was your brief with Jameson too. But he killed himself. Well, I'll tell you something: I'm not going to serve time for this. I want you to know that, so whatever happens you won't be able to say to the media that you didn't realise what would happen.'

He turned away from her. It was a gesture of rejection.

'I'll see you later, Mason,' she said. 'Don't give up hope.'

He ignored her and again she was reminded of Watch.

She made her way along the hospital corridor towards Tom's office. He was on the phone and waved her to a chair.

' . . . about lunch-time,' he was saying. 'Yes, of
course I will. What? A case? Good God no . . .
Anyway, I'll pick something up . . . Yes, fine . . . all
right . . . 'Bye.'

He put down the phone and smiled at Anne. 'My
mother.' He nodded to the phone. 'Wants me to
bring a case of wine. I'm only going to be there one
night – and she drinks gin.'

She wondered if he was going to repeat his
weekend invitation. He didn't, but again she was
aware of that slight feeling of tension.

Fanny Fielder was a professional portraitist and
someone Anne would have liked to meet. Tom had
shown her a portrait she had done of him and she
had thought it brilliant. It seemed to bring out
characteristics she herself had noticed: his restless
energy, his easy but non-committal manner. Yet
behind his eyes there was something his mother
had missed, as though experiences had etched
themselves there which told of unhappiness. The
obvious cause was his former wife, Stephanie. Anne
had met her once or twice and hadn't enjoyed the
meetings.

'How's Chitty?' he said.

'Much the same. He's threatening suicide again.'

'Worried?'

'I suppose he's as secure as possible but no one
can ever be absolutely secure.'

'The problem with Chitty is the usual one:
psychotics who threaten suicide usually carry it out.'

'That's if he is psychotic.'

'Granted. Something else . . . I spoke to our press officer and to our leader. The press officer hasn't heard of the series Sophie Lennox told you about but he's going to inquire for us. Roger is in the same mood he was in the other day: worried that something is going to happen that will make life unpleasant for him.'

The phone rang. Tom answered it, then handed it to her, 'Gatelodge for you.'

She picked up the receiver. 'Yes. Who? Could you hold for a moment?' She turned to Tom. 'Lily Benson, the dead girl's mother, is at the gatelodge. She wants to see me.'

'Have you spoken to her at all?'

'No. Should I?'

'There's no reason why not. She probably just wants to ask about Chitty.'

Anne crossed to the gatelodge which was in the old covered way that dated back to the middle of the nineteenth century and where the horse-drawn prison wagons had unloaded their cargoes of convicts, all ironed and chained. Standing amid the modern bustle was the woman she had watched in court, but there was a subtle difference in her now. She was no longer so wretched looking, in fact she was quite handsome.

Anne introduced herself and Lily said, 'Is there somewhere we can talk, doctor?'

'Can you tell me what it's about?'

She indicated the movement of people around them and said, 'I'd rather not talk here.'

There was something pathetic yet eager about her that triggered Anne's emotional receptors. What if it had been Hilly, not Sandra Benson, who had disappeared? She had thought about this several times in court as the case unfolded.

'Would you like a coffee?' she said.

'That would be fine.'

Anne took her back to her room.

'How are you, Mrs Benson?' she said.

'I'm well, thank you, doctor.'

'Sugar?'

'I don't take it. Sandra used to love it. She'd take three in coffee.'

'Young people often do. How can I help you?'

'We've had a meeting about Sandra,' Lily said. 'In the village. At Mrs Drayton's house.'

'I've seen her in court. She has a rather grand house, hasn't she? Isn't it listed?'

'She was grand once, too, but not any more. Not since her son was killed in the Gulf War.'

'What was the meeting about?'

'About looking for Sandra. The village wants to help. Lots of people came. We've formed working parties.'

'But where are you going to start?' Anne said. 'If she's alive she could be anywhere, she might even have left the country.'

'Oh, no, we're not looking for her alive. For a long time I wouldn't believe she was dead, but I do now.'

'You mean from what you've heard in court?'

'That and something else?'

'What was the something else?'

'Sandra spoke to me.'

It was said, to Anne's ears, with complete conviction. 'You heard her voice?'

'Just her voice. There was nothing else.'

'And she said?'

'Find me.'

'Find me?'

Lily heard the doubt in Anne's tone. 'You may not believe it but that's what she said.'

'Well, I . . .'

'Doctors don't know everything!'

'That's true.'

Lily had flushed with anger, but she controlled herself and said, 'That's what made me change my mind.'

'Her speaking to you?'

'Yes. She wants me to find her and I want to find her and give her a proper burial. We must mourn. And we can't mourn if we can't bury our dead.' Her voice had risen. 'I started looking even before the meeting, but Samuel Chitty told me to get off his land and Mrs Drayton found me and took me into her home. That's how it all began. And then the people coming for the meeting. And

86

me making scones and a cake . . . Sandra didn't like scones but she ate the cake sometimes . . . Fruit cake . . . Barry used to love it . . . And the Admiral said how much he liked the cake. He said it reminded him of his wife's because she used rum in hers and I used it in mine instead of brandy because it was a naval fruit cake and rum is traditional in the Navy and—' As her speech grew more rapid her Hampshire accent, which had not been discernible at first, grew more pronounced.

'Mrs Benson, I'm sorry to interrupt you but I was wondering what it was you wanted to see me about?'

Lily checked her outpouring and said, 'I want you to ask Mason Chitty where he put her.'

'Where he put your daughter?'

'Where he hid her after he killed her. I don't want to know how he killed her or what he did to her. I don't want to *know* those things. I've thought and thought and hated him so much that if I could have killed him I would. Or his mother. Or his brother. Killed them in the most horrible ways. But what I want to know now is where he hid her so I can find her and mourn.'

Anne said, 'I don't think I can do that. I'm a doctor. I'm treating him for . . . well, for illness . . . and he's in the middle of a case . . .'

'But he's the only one who knows. That's what the Admiral said. He said if anyone knows where she is it's Mason Chitty.'

'I realise that. But I can't ask him questions like that. In any case, his lawyer wouldn't allow it.'

'You won't help me then?'

'I can't help you. Not that way. I'm really sorry, Mrs Benson.'

Lily stood up and went towards the door. Anne escorted her to the car-park and, as Lily was getting into the car, she said, 'You must have known Mason Chitty.'

'Of course I did. He lived in the village.'

'Did you see him much? In the pub, perhaps?'

'No, the Chittys never went there.' She spoke grudgingly.

'Do you know if he ever tried to commit suicide?'

'Not that I heard of.' She began to close the car door. 'I wish someone would kill him,' she said.

'Mr Watch is asleep!' Hilly said as Anne opened the door of the house. 'He's been sleeping all day.'

Anne hugged her and gave her a bag of food to carry. They went into the kitchen.

'I expect he needs it,' Anne said. 'Don't forget he came all the way from Lesotho.'

'I asked Grandpa where Lesotho is and he says it's in the middle of South Africa. I thought it was a real country.'

'It is, darling. And Grandpa's right. It lies in the middle of South Africa and how it got there is a long and complicated story which I'm not going into now.'

'Anne?' Henry's voice rose from his basement flat.

'I'm here.'

'I'm coming up to have a drink.'

Anne turned to Hilly. 'Have you eaten?'

'Grandpa made a stew. Yuk.'

'I'll make us some cheese and tomato on toast later.'

Hilly went upstairs as Henry arrived in Anne's kitchen.

'There's some stew left,' he said.

'I had a large lunch,' Anne lied.

Henry's pipe gave an irritated gurgle. 'Pity, it was expensive beef.'

'Did Watch have any?'

'No, that's why there's some left.'

She poured herself a glass of wine and her father a whisky and soda.

Henry said, 'I'm slightly concerned about him.'

In her father's lexicon, 'slightly concerned' meant worried stiff.

'Hasn't he eaten anything?'

'Mush.'

'Mush?'

'Oh, you know, Hilly's breakfast stuff. That mouse stuff.'

'Muesli. Well, that's healthy.'

'You can't have it twice or three times a day. It'll kill you.'

'I'm glad he's eaten something.'

'Wouldn't eat any proper food.'

'I think I know why.'

'I hope you're going to share it with me.'

'Role reversal. You were his employer for all those years and he looked after you. He went on doing that even when you'd retired. Now you are looking after him. Imagine you've been a bank clerk for years and years and for some reason you leave the bank and find that the bank manager you worked for all this time is suddenly working for you in some domestic capacity.'

'I hate bank managers. I'd kick his arse for him. But I accept what you're saying. I can see that, and I agree. But there's something deeper, I think. Something's happened to change Watch.'

'It's probably all those nieces and nephews he's been supporting.'

'Maybe. Anyway, I took him to the law courts and showed him round. He didn't seem frightfully interested. So I took him out and bought him some real clothes. Can't go walking round Kingstown with someone in a gold-and-purple tracksuit. How was your day?'

There were times when she wished her father still lived in Africa but this wasn't one of them. It was good to have him there in the evenings. Good to have him say, how was your day? Good to be in communication with someone other than a member of the prison staff.

She told him about Lily and, surprisingly, he said, 'She's right. She must mourn. And you can't really mourn if you don't know what's happened to your child's body. I knew a woman in Maseru once whose son – probably much the age of Mrs Benson's daughter – was killed in a ritual murder. That's what the police said. The point is, they never found him. If it was a ritual killing his body would have been cut up into pieces and some of it would have been eaten and some kept for *muti*, the magic medicine. But his mother wanted to find him and started looking for him up on the slopes of Thaba Bosio. She searched for about ten years. Used to take a pick and dig. Went quite dotty and died up there in a snow storm. Strange place Thaba Bosio. Lots of people died there. It's not called the Mountain of Night for nothing.'

'Some of the things Mrs Benson said sounded a bit dotty to me. She says she hears Sandra's voice and she wishes someone would kill Mason Chitty.'

'I think you're mixing with the wrong sort of people.'

She laughed, then grew serious. 'The trouble is, I don't really know if I believe Mason or not.'

'It's not your business to believe him or not to believe him, it's your business to bring him to trial fit enough to stand it.'

'I know, I know, but . . .'

'It always comes back to Jameson, doesn't it?'

'Well, I wasn't sure whether I believed him either and look what happened.'

10

'Right, then . . . sorry about the weather, but thank you all for coming.'

There was a cold wind blowing from the north-east and it had brought a fine drizzle with it. Vice-Admiral Sir Peter Pattinson stood on slightly higher ground than the others as he addressed the first working party. Apart from himself there were Lily Benson and Mike Treagust and Elizabeth Drayton. That was all.

They were at the bottom of what had once been the gallops. Half a mile ahead of them were the big gates which the Chittys had put up when they bought the land from Elizabeth Drayton. And further on, to the right, was their house.

The Admiral looked at his watch. 'I make it just eighteen hundred hours.'

Lily thought how much the English gentleman he appeared. He was wearing an old pair of yellow corduroy trousers which had lost the nap on both knees, an equally old tweed sports jacket of a Findhorn pattern, and a tweed cap in which were stuck half a dozen trout flies. This was how Barry would have wanted to dress, she thought, if he had lived. He had always wanted to take up fishing. In

Sir Peter's hands were a blackthorn walking stick and a map.

By comparison, Mike Treagust was dressed in climbing boots, climbing trousers, a South Pole kagoul and a woollen beanie.

Elizabeth Drayton wore her long cloak and this time her white hair was covered by a scarf.

Kenny had been there earlier but he had brrrroooom-brrroomed away on his invisible motorbike, much to everyone's relief.

The Admiral said, 'Because this is the first working party I thought we should make a reconnaissance before starting the search proper. See the lie of the land. See what we need. Obviously we are going to need walking sticks.' He held up his. 'We'll need them for prodding the ground if we see a disturbed path. That's what we're looking for. Anything that doesn't seem right. Nettles that grow up in a place where otherwise there are none . . . that's always a good place to investigate. Next time we'll bring tapes to mark off areas like the police do. We will have to be vigilant because Sandra disappeared last autumn.'

He held up his map. 'Mrs Drayton's been kind enough to give me this survey map which covers both farms and I'm going to have photocopies made for us and for the other working parties. I took it to my friendly policeman and he asked his officers to shade in the areas they searched on the Chitty land so we can see where they've been. We can meet after a recce and mark the places we've searched and discuss where next to go. All right?'

It seemed to be all right with everyone.

'If any of you have any ideas I'd be glad to hear them now. Especially from Mrs Benson.' He smiled at her expectantly but she lowered her eyes.

'What about the river?' Mike Treagust said. 'Shouldn't we look at that?'

'The police had frogmen in for days and they found nothing. No, we've got to look near the Chitty boundary. It would have been too dangerous to carry Sandra far from Chitty land.'

'You're assuming he buried her on Elizabeth's land?' Treagust said.

'We can't assume a damn thing. We just don't know. We can't search the Chittys' land because they've refused to allow us. Mrs Chitty said the police have gone over it exhaustively and that's that. Can't blame her really. No, we've got to search Mrs Drayton's land because it's nearest. And if you look at it logically, anyone carrying a body would have made for a gate, so the areas near the gates would be best.'

'Fine, Peter,' Treagust said.

The Admiral looked at him irritably. 'Let's move off then.'

Elizabeth Drayton said to Lily, 'I'm going back to the house but Sir Peter will look after you. Come in for coffee when you get back.'

Lily was surprised. She had thought Elizabeth would have been on every recce – Barry had used that word too.

'You ready, Mrs Benson?' Sir Peter said.

'Yes, thank you.'

The three of them began to walk up the gallops. Near the gate a smaller track veered away keeping to Drayton land. It was rough and even though Lily had put on a sensible pair of walking shoes she found the surface difficult. I'm unfit, she thought, I can't walk properly any more.

Sir Peter said, 'We'll get off this track in a bit and the country flattens out. You'll find it easier then.'

They went on another half a mile or so, then came to the top of the Downs. They paused and watched a lorry grinding along what seemed to be a private road.

'What about there?' Treagust pointed beyond the lorry.

What he was pointing at and what the lorry was making for was a huge waste infill.

'The tip?' the Admiral said.

'That's the place I'd look.'

'The police have been over it with a fine-tooth comb. Anyway, it's several miles from the stables where they think she was killed. No one could have carried her that far.'

'He could have taken her in his Land-Rover.'

'There's no road to it from the farmhouse. Not

96

even a Land-Rover could make it. But the police searched the Land-Rover. No blood in it. No evidence of it being used.'

He turned to Lily. 'You must forgive me for talking about Sandra like this. I wish there was some other way.'

'I know,' she said.

They went on. The clouds darkened and the wind increased. The Admiral stopped again, took a small pair of powerful binoculars from his jacket pocket and began searching the gorse and scrubland away to their right. 'I thought I saw something but I couldn't have.'

They went on for another few hundred yards. They had come down onto a flattish area. The river was to their left, the Downs to their right, and at the foot of the Downs was a new barbed-wire fence.

'Chittys' fence,' Sir Peter said.

'This all used to be Elizabeth's,' Mike Treagust said, 'until she sold—' He stopped abruptly. 'I thought I saw something too.' He pointed to the dark shape of the Down which loomed up on their right. 'Near the top.'

He raised his monocular and stared at the grassy slope.

'Anything?'

'Nothing.'

'Right,' Sir Peter said. 'I think this is where we should start when we get the tapes. I'll tell the others. This is where it's most likely. We're near the Chitty fence. There are stands of trees. There's the coppice over there. And all that rough, broken ground with the boulders. The stables are just out of sight.'

'It's very big – and rough.' Lily was looking at a flat area about half a mile in length and perhaps three hundred yards wide with all the features Sir Peter had mentioned.

He said, 'This was a wheat field until last year. We'll go over it inch by inch.'

They went to a stand of trees occupying about forty acres.

'Let's split up. What we want is to make a rough plan of the wood for the others. We can search this thoroughly first and move on later.'

The three of them set off about fifty yards apart. Lily wasn't sure what she was supposed to be looking for. The ground was covered in leaves and there was heavy scrub between beeches and oaks. Every now and then root balls reared up higher than Lily herself where trees lay on their sides still uncleared from the two great storms of recent years.

Soon she could only see the others as shadows in the dusk. Clearly the two men were not in the least apprehensive about being in the wood, but she felt lost, almost abandoned. Above her the big trees clashed in the wind. Sandra could be anywhere here and they would never find her. She could be hidden under fallen timber and buried in deep leaf mould. Lily remembered films from her childhood: the grasping branches in Disney's *Snow White*; the graveyard scene in *Great Expectations*. When she was little, living in the family home in Portsmouth, she had seen the films with her father. Being a policeman on the beat, he worked at odd hours and liked to take his small daughter to the cinema when he was free. 'You mustn't be frightened,' he would tell her. 'It's only pictures.' But at night she would lie in bed and the films would unreel in her mind and she would be afraid.

She heard a sound and thought a fox or a rabbit had started at her feet. Then she felt something grasp her arm. In terror, she looked down and saw a hand. The hand was joined to an arm, the arm to a body, the body to a face.

It belonged to the horse coper, Mitchell.

He released her. His sallow face was framed by his shock of greasy black hair. He was wearing a single earring.

'I been watching,' he said, 'I been up there on the tops.'

She heard someone crashing through the undergrowth. Sir Peter came towards them.

'What the hell are you playing at, Mitchell? Are you all right, Mrs Benson?'

'Yes. Mr Mitchell says he was watching us. He was up on the Downs.'

'Not watching you,' Mitchell said. 'Watching out in case someone was there. I thought I seen someone.'

'Who?'

'Can't say. But someone running.'

Treagust arrived. 'What's going on?'

'We've been under surveillance,' Sir Peter said. 'Mitchell saw someone from the hill.'

Tom Melville said, 'I haven't drunk so much real coffee as opposed to instant for . . . oh, for years.' He accepted a cup from Anne and sipped at the smoking surface. It was something of a ritual these days that when morning surgery was over and before they went to their respective offices and prepared their psychiatric court reports – which meant listening to inmates for hours at a time – Anne invited Tom to her room for coffee.

It had become a place for informal discussion about prisoners, and sometimes personal matters.

Like this morning.

'How's Chitty?' Tom said.

'Not talking today. He talked yesterday. Not today.'

'Are you worried?'

'I wish I could answer that. He's asked about liver damage several times. It's as though he's depending on that for what he didn't achieve with the paracetamol.'

'I know what you're thinking.'

'Well, it's true. Jameson talked about suicide.'

'A lot of them do. By the way, I spoke to Holroyd last night. He says he's checked with the major production companies and there are no plans for a TV series on prisons. Holroyd hasn't even found out where the girl is working – that's if she *is* working.'

'Why would she go to all this trouble if she wasn't working?'

'That was my line. Holroyd thinks she may be trying to set up a series. Anyway he's still trying to trace her.'

'And when he finds her?'

'We'll talk to her. Or I will if you like. Just see what she's up to. It'd be interesting to know if anyone in Stepton has been approached by a TV company. If anyone has, you can be sure we'll also be in the frame.'

'Why don't I ask around? It's something I've wanted to do, if only to find out more about Mason and whether he was a suicide risk before.'

'Why not? It's legitimate business. We need to know.'

He looked at his watch and drained his mug. 'Thanks for the coffee. I must go.'

As he reached the door she said, 'Is that weekend invitation still open for Hilly and me?'

'Of course it is.'

'I'm still not absolutely sure, but Watch is being a bit of a problem and I thought it might be better to leave him with my father and let the two of them get used to each other again. I think three of us are a bit much for him.'

'You suit yourself. It would be nice for me if you came.'

Oh Sandra I feel so ashamed. I should have been here last night sitting in this chair.

I was late getting home, love, and I knew that if I went straight to bed I would sleep – and I did.

Perhaps it was the whisky. Elizabeth had asked us for coffee but when we came back from the Downs she said we could have either. The Admiral had whisky but Mike Treagust said his wife would have made Ovaltine, so he left. Mitchell didn't stay either, which pleased Elizabeth.

So the three of us had a whisky. Elizabeth was charming. She's different from the person I used to see in the village. And she seems to like my company.

My love, we walked over the area where the Admiral thinks we should look. It's very difficult. There are woods and that boggy place we saw once on a walk, and those old dane-holes. And Mitchell says we were being watched by someone.

We talked a lot about you. Elizabeth remembers you well. Such a pretty girl, she said. And then the Admiral brought me home in his car. He's been so nice – always asking if I'm all right.

I didn't ask him in. I wonder if I should have?

If only you would talk to me again and tell me where you are.

11

A fine rain was falling as Anne drove off the main Chichester – Kingstown road and took a lane with high hedgerows signposted to Stepton. She had been to the village several times since coming to live in Kingstown but knew nothing more of it than the Mayfly pub with its terrace that overlooked the river. She had last visited it with Clive Parker, who had wanted to marry her, and she had sat in the winter sunshine in a heavy coat, certain that her nose was red, and told him it wasn't going to happen.

Now, as she drove past the pub she could hardly remember what he looked like. This had been a typical rebound affair. She had met him after her lover, Paul – Hilly's father – had been killed in an accident, and Clive had taken her over when she needed someone. He had also lent her money free of interest when she and her father bought the house in Kingstown. Her affair with him, she had soon begun to realise, had been based on gratitude. So she had repaid the money and had sat in the cold here in Stepton and told him she wouldn't marry him.

She passed the Mayfly, stopped in a small lay-by, consulted a map, then went on. The village

103

streets were narrow and she just missed being hit by a delivery van as she turned past the shop.

She drove away from the village and began to climb the Downs, and then saw the house. It was at the end of a bare drive. At one time, she thought, it might have been lined by trees but now it was just a roadway that lay between tussocks of grass.

She had never seen Ridge farmhouse before and it was unlovely. Part of it was flint and part concrete which was covered in patches of dark-green algae. It was surrounded by glaring yellow rape fields and few trees. There was a garden but it was overgrown by weeds and grass.

She rang the bell and the door was opened instantly as though she had been expected. She realised that anyone in the house could see the car coming up the drive a mile away.

'Yes?'

She was looking at Florence Chitty, whom she had last seen in court. Her face was thin and heavily lined. She stood with her arms folded across her narrow chest and looked at Anne as though she had never seen her before.

'Mrs Chitty, I'm Dr Vernon from the prison.'

'I know who you are.'

There was something about her that made Anne feel uneasy. It was a feeling she had had in court, too: the unforgiving quality of the woman's dark-blue eyes.

'I'm sorry to bother you but I wondered if we could talk.'

'Talk? What about?'

She made it sound as though the request was an impertinence. Anne had not heard her say much before and now realised her accent was not from West Sussex or Hampshire. The vowels were flattened and there was a nasal twang.

'About Mason.'

'What about Mason?'

'Could we go inside, do you think? It might be easier for us there.'

'You're not welcome in my home.'

'I'm sorry you feel that way. Why?'

'Can't you think why? My son lies in a hospital bed because of you.'

'Now hang on a moment, Mrs Chitty . . .'

'I don't want to talk to you.'

'I'm trying to help Mason. I'm—'

'Is giving him poisons helping him?' She turned and said something in a low voice. Mason's brother, Samuel, appeared at her side.

'Mother don't feel like talking to you,' he said.

He was of medium height, with his mother's thin face. He was as unlike Mason as it was possible to be, Anne thought. His dark hair was thick and peppered with grey. He spoke slowly and moved slowly.

Anne said, 'I can understand that, but if you believe that Mason was given—'

'She don't want to hear no more about Mason,' Samuel said.

'I'll go then. But first would you answer a question: has anyone from TV approached you about a programme concerning Mason?'

Mrs Chitty said, 'If they had we wouldn't tell you. It ain't your business.'

Anne got into her car, feeling angry and humiliated. She drove down the bare hillside and entered the village. She knew the Chittys must be going through a traumatic time with Mason standing trial and his attempt at suicide, but even so they seemed unnecessarily unpleasant.

She turned the corner by the village shop. There was a sudden blurred movement near the shop front. She swung the wheel hard to the left and felt a bump as the blur and the right mudguard collided. Then, as he fell, she saw that the blur was a man.

She ran to him. He was a small man with a young-old face and he was sitting in the road rubbing his right shoulder. A woman came out of the shop and stared at her.

'I didn't see him!' Anne said. She bent to him. 'I'm a doctor. Don't move. Can you tell me where you're hurt?'

In reply the man pushed himself to his feet.

'Brrroom-brrroom' he said, went off up the road and vanished round a corner.

Anne looked after him in bewilderment. The

woman came down the steps of the shop and said,
'Kenny's always getting into accidents. Never seem
to hurt him.'

'But I must do something about him! There may
be damage and—'

'You couldn't damage Kenny. Need a tank for
that.' There was a kind of pride in the way she said
it.

'I must see that he's all right.'

'He'll be with his mum, Mrs Elkins. She'll see to
him if he needs seeing to.'

'Where do they live?'

The woman gave her directions.

The council house was one of a small group, each
precisely the same as its neighbour and only given
character by its garden. The garden outside number
seven was neatly kept and had recently been dug
over.

Anne knocked at the door. It was opened by an
untidy woman in her sixties who, on this chilly day,
was wearing a short-sleeved blouse which showed
off her upper arms to disadvantage.

'Mrs Elkins?'

'You the one who knocked into Kenny? The shop
just phoned you was on your way. You a doctor?'

'Yes. I came to find out how he was.'

'Come in, doctor.'

There was the throb of respect in her tone with
which Anne had become familiar. Sometimes it did
her good when she was feeling less than her usual

optimistic self, but mostly she tried to ignore it.

In the front room an ironing board was set up and the TV was on to a game show with the sound turned down. Mrs Elkins scooped up an armful of clothing from a chair covered in grey uncut moquette, and said, 'Won't you sit down, doctor?'

'I'd rather see Kenny.'

'Kenny's having a wash.'

'I really must find out—'

'There's nothing wrong with him. This happens all the time. If it isn't cars it's cycles. If it isn't cycles it's people. Kenny bangs into things on that motorbike of his.'

'Motorbike? I didn't see a motorbike.'

'It's not a motorbike you can see, if you get my meaning. It's only in his head. He's been riding it since he was a nipper. He's forty-two now, though you wouldn't know it.'

'I still think I should have him examined,' Anne said.

Mrs Elkins brushed back a long tress of grey hair. 'You leave Kenny to me, doctor, he's my boy. Now I'm going to give us some coffee.'

Anne watched the silently quacking faces on the game show until Mrs Elkins returned with a mug of instant coffee.

'You don't want to fret about Kenny,' she said. 'He's all right as long as he's got his blessed bike.'

'Does he ride it all the time?'

'Always. And always uses it when he's running

errands. I say to him, Kenny would you go down to the shop and get me a tin of baked beans and he gets his bike and off he goes. Broom-broommm . . . And that's what happened today. I'd sent him for some sugar and you were coming the other way, Olive says, from the Chittys' place.'

'Who's Olive?'

'She has the shop. You spoke to her.'

'And she knew I'd come from the Chittys' farm?'

'Olive knows everything in the village. Can't keep a blessed thing from her. But seeing you wouldn't be difficult. Her windows look up the road to the Chittys' drive. She must have seen you going up and coming down.'

Anne took a mouthful of coffee and wished she hadn't. 'I went to talk to them about Mason.'

'What about Mason.'

'Just a chat. To tell them how he's getting on.'

'How is he getting on?'

'Fine. Well . . . as fine as you can be when you're on trial and in prison.' Even that, she knew, was a lie.

'I'd of said Samuel was more likely to do a murder than Mason. Oh yes, doctor, much more likely.'

'We don't know Mason did commit a murder. He hasn't been tried yet. I've heard that he and Samuel didn't get on.'

'That Samuel . . . well, he's a strange lad.'

Anne registered that like Kenny, men in their forties were lads or boys to Mrs Elkins. This was the result, she thought, of having a son who would always be a child, no matter how old he became.

'How's he strange?'

'Well, he's a man for himself. Never comes down to the village. Always goes out by the other road, the one by the tip. And he's no countryman, not like Mason was. Shouldn't say "was" I suppose.'

'No, not until we hear the verdict.'

'Used to drive a taxi in Kingstown, Samuel did, even after he got rich. Still does from time to time.'

'How did he get rich?'

'They want us to believe it was farming, but it wasn't. It was that rubbish tip. Lorries come from all over now. Worth a fortune that is.'

'Brrrooomm-Brrrooom . . .' Kenny came into the room on his bike.

'Don't you go getting oil on my good carpet,' his mother said.

'Brrrooom-brrrooom . . .'

'How are you, Kenny?' Anne said.

'All right.'

'Are you sure?'

'All right.'

'You going to do some diggin'?' his mother said.

'Broommm.'

'That's a good boy. You go and get the spade.'

Kenny put the bike in gear and drove out of the room.

'Loves diggin',' Mrs Elkins said. 'More coffee?'

'No thanks. I must be going.'

'Do you think he did it?'

'Mason? No, I don't. Do you? I mean, does the village?'

'They say how did her blood really get on him.'

'Mrs Elkins, can I ask you something else? Did Mason . . . did you ever hear that Mason had tried to commit suicide at any time?'

'Suicide? What give you that idea?'

'Well, it's just that he's in a . . . a difficult physical – and mental – condition at the moment. You know, depressed. I wondered if he had a history of that kind of thing . . . so that we know what to watch for . . .'

The sentence ended lamely and she could see a questioning look in Mrs Elkins's eyes.

'You think he will?'

'Commit suicide? Good heavens no, but I feel we should know everything we can about his past just in case he tries.'

'Well, I dunno.' She laughed, but her laugh contained no humour. 'If you start life as a girl and then become a boy, I expect you'd be capable of anything.'

12

When Anne left the prison that evening the weather
had improved and the sun was out. Henry was in
her kitchen when she arrived home and was staring
unhappily at his cookbook. He was dressed in what
she thought of now as his cooking gear: a collarless
white shirt, dusty morning trousers which he had
once worn at formal functions, and patent-leather
dancing pumps still covered by a faint layer of
Africa's mud and cow dung. He was also wearing
her frilly yellow apron.

'What's a béchamel sauce?' he said.

'A white sauce.'

'Why the hell don't they say so?'

'What're you making?'

'Cauliflower cheese. Watch used to love cauliflower cheese.'

'Has he eaten anything?'

'Not much. I made him scrambled eggs and bacon
with toast for lunch and he hardly touched it.'

'Be careful when you make the sauce. If you don't
keep stirring it goes lumpy.'

'Oh ye of little faith . . . Just pour me a whisky,
please.'

'I have to go to Stepton. I thought we might all

go. Get Watch out of the house.'

'Why Stepton?'

She told him what had happened to Kenny that morning.

He frowned and said, 'An imaginary motorbike?'

'He's got learning difficulties.'

'In my day that was called retarded but never mind. You sure he wasn't hurt?'

'No, I'm not sure. That's why I want to go back; to make sure.'

'Right, we'll go in the Rover.'

'No! In my car.'

'It's too small.'

'Father!'

'Oh, all right.'

'How's Watch been, apart from not eating?'

Henry wiped his hands on the apron and she mentally placed it in the washing machine. 'He's started to give little hints that things weren't as we thought. When we split up, i.e. when I came back here, he went off to live with his sister in Maseru.'

'We knew that.'

'Yes, but his sister was living with another man and her children were living in the house as well and when Watch arrived things must have been different from what he had expected.'

'His sister was a widow, wasn't she?'

'I met her husband before he died. Rotten bugger. Didn't do any work that I could discover. She, on the other hand, washed and cooked and ironed and cleaned for people in Maseru.'

'Did he tell you who the other man was?'

'He called him "the cook" that's all. But it's apparent that Watch and the cook didn't get on.'

'Maybe that's why he came over here.'

'We'll find out in time,' Henry said. 'I'll go and get him off his bed.'

While he was down in his own flat Anne set the kitchen to rights and called Hilly. They drove out to Stepton. The village was looking beautiful. Henry said, 'If you don't look at the TV aerials and the telephone poles nothing's changed since Jane Austen wrote about places like this.'

'Who's Jane Austen?' Hilly said.

'A writer,' Anne said. 'We've got books of hers at home.'

Hilly was sitting beside Watch at the back. Since they had left home fifteen minutes before, he had not spoken. Now he said, 'Motorbike.'

Anne slammed on the brakes and Kenny came into view. She got out. Kenny was about to swerve round her but she stopped him.

'Are you all right, Kenny?'

'All right,' he said.

'Won't you let another doctor examine you?'

'Brrriiim-Brrriiimmm . . .' Kenny said, changing the engine note slightly, then he went racing up the street.

'Learning difficulties?' Henry said.

Anne ignored him. 'He looks all right, doesn't he?' Then she turned to Watch. 'How did you know it was a motorbike?'

'When I was a boy I too rode eh-motorbike like that.'

'Like what?' Hilly said.

'Never mind, darling, I'll explain later.'

The evening had turned warm and still and they went to the pub terrace. There was a hatch of flies on the water and trout were rising lazily.

Watch asked for a brandy. Hilly said, 'Can I have a packet of crisps?'

Abruptly Watch got to his feet. 'I'll get you crisps.'

Anne said, 'No, no Watch, why should you—?'

But Watch was not listening. He came back a few moments later with three packets of crisps, two pork pies, a large slab of chocolate and another brandy.

He handed the crisps around and began to demolish the pies, the chocolate and the brandies. He was taking a mouthful of his second glass of brandy when a woman came up to their table and stopped in front of Anne.

She said, 'We're going to find her without your help, Dr Vernon!'

Lily Benson was wearing a smart red dress, a scarf around her throat, and high-heeled shoes. Her face had lost some of its gaunt angularity.

Beyond her, a man was standing by a table, holding a couple of glasses and looking towards them.

116

'I'm glad, Mrs Benson,' Anne said. 'You know I'd help if I could.'

'I don't want your help now.' She turned and brushed into Watch, apologised and went across to join the man.

'Who was that?' Henry said.

'The murdered girl's mother.'

'What was she talking about?'

'Well, she—'

'Mummy!'

'I'm talking to Grandpa, darling.'

'It's Mr Watch.'

Anne and Henry swung round. If a dark-skinned person could be said to have gone pale, Watch had gone pale. His face had taken on a greyish colour. His brandy glass was trembling in his hands.

'What's the matter?' Anne said.

Watch said nothing for a few moments, then he began to speak softly in Sesotho, the language of his people.

'What's the matter, old man?' Henry said.

The strange torrent of words continued.

Anne said, 'I think we should get him home.'

All the way back to Kingstown Watch continued to speak Sesotho. Occasionally he would go silent, then he would start again. Hilly, who was sitting in the back with him, moved as far away as possible but he did not seem to notice. At the house he went to his room and they heard the door close.

Anne looked questioningly at her father.

'God knows,' he said. 'I've seen him like this only a few times in forty years. I remember once a felon tried to attack me in court after I'd sentenced him and Watch restrained him. Well . . . restrained is putting it mildly. He hit him with one of those big glass desk sets that contain heavy inkwells, and knocked him cold. Afterwards he sat about talking to himself and . . .'

'What are you going to do?' Anne cut across her father's reminiscences.

'What *can* we do?'

'I knew something was going to happen the moment you said Watch was coming to stay. This just isn't his scene and I think he's unhappy.'

'If he were unhappy he'd go back to Lesotho, he wouldn't stay here.'

'He may not have any money to go back. Did he have a return ticket?'

'You don't ask your guests that kind of question.'

'I'm going to find out,' Anne said. 'He doesn't eat. He spends ages in his room. He doesn't take part in the family. He must be unhappy. And if he's unhappy then we should help him get back.'

'Maybe he doesn't want to go back. He's only just arrived.'

'Well, I'm going to ask him.'

'He'll think you're trying to get rid of him.'

Hilly tugged her dress. 'He's making funny noises.'

'Who?'

'Mr Watch. Listen!'

They went to the head of Henry's staircase. From Watch's room came a series of clicks as though he were playing a game of snooker. They stopped. Then they started again.

'I'm going down,' Anne said.

Henry followed her.

'Watch,' she called through the door. There was no answer.

'I'm coming in, old man,' Henry said.

He turned the door handle and went in. Anne followed. Hilly stood at the back craning round the doorpost. Watch was seated on the floor. In his hand he had a few yellowish objects which Anne could not identify. He threw them underhand at the wall. They struck and fell back on the floor. This was the noise they had heard.

Henry turned to Anne and Hilly and indicated that they should get out of the room. He then went back in and closed the door.

Anne stood uncertainly for a moment, then said, 'Come on, darling. Bed.'

She had expected a fight, but Hilly went up meekly. When she was in her bath she said, 'Mr Watch went funny.'

'We know that,' Anne said, soaping her back. 'What we don't know is why.'

'The lady made him go funny.'

'Which lady?'

'The one at the pub, the one who spoke to you.

119

He went funny when she touched him.'

Anne recalled Lily Benson brushing past Watch and apologising to him.

'His eyes went white and his face went funny.'

Her father came up the stairs. 'Anne!'

'Coming.'

Henry was standing in the middle of her kitchen. 'He's throwing the bones,' he said.

'Throwing bones?'

'Throwing *the* bones. That's the expression. It's something done in African necromancy. People who throw the bones can "see" things. The bones "tell" them things. Like fortune tellers here who read cards or tea-leaves.'

'What have the bones told Watch?'

'God knows. I'll talk to him later. I wonder where he got them.'

'What?'

'The bones.'

'At any butcher shop, I imagine.'

'Not these. They're human vertebrae. Much more magic in human bones.'

'I don't believe you!'

'Oh, yes. Don't forget that for years Lesotho was a place of ritual murder. These are probably very old human bones. He may have bought them or they could have been handed down.'

'But he's never done this before that you know of?'

'Not that I know of, but that doesn't signify much.

120

He could have been throwing the bones morning, noon and night and if he did it in private I'd never have known.'

She held up her hand. 'Don't tell me any more.'

'As a child you must have come across Africans throwing the bones. Or something similar.'

'If I did I've thankfully forgotten about it. I really don't want to hear any more. I think I've heard too much already.'

She went to say good-night to Hilly.

'How would you like to go to Wales this weekend?' she said.

There is no way to stop the crying. It comes unexpectedly. It comes now as Lily is cleaning the kitchen cupboard. She has cleaned the sink and the splashback, the walls, the worktops and the table.

She has cleaned these a hundred times since Sandra's death. Now she's moved onto the long larder cupboard.

Barry had refused to throw it out when they'd bought the house. He said he's refurbish it and he'd just started working on it when he died. Eventually she'd finished it. And he was right, it looked as good as new.

Oh Barry . . .

And then she realises, with a start, that she is crying for him – something she hasn't done for years – and she stops cleaning and stops crying and goes to Sandra's room.

She sits on the hard chair and strokes Sandra's gloves.

Everything is organised, my love. The working parties go out separately. Ours is going out again this weekend. Betty says she'll come this time so that will make an extra woman. It's a bit much with just the men. I mean they walk so fast. Except the Admiral. He waits and looks after me.

We've put the tapes up. Red tapes with little alleys between them. We have meetings most evenings now, mostly at the Mayfly. Then the others come in and tell us how much they've done and the Admiral marks it all off on his map.

She sits in Sandra's room for an hour and in all that time she does not cry.

I'm getting better, she thinks. I'm not going mad.

13

Tintern Abbey, grim and forbidding in the grey light, came up on their right and Tom said, 'At least you can see the things at close quarters, not like Stonehenge.'

The three of them were in his old Land-Rover and Anne's bottom was numb from the hard front seat. Behind her sat Hilly with Tom's miniature dachshund, Beanie. Hilly had formed a close relationship with the dog when it had had a fractured back, and had helped Tom with the physiotherapy which had returned Beanie almost to normal. And normal for a tiny dachshund – as Anne and Hilly had discovered – meant sitting and sleeping on laps and generally running the show. As long as Hilly had Beanie Anne knew she didn't have to worry about her boredom factor.

'What about lunch?' Tom said. 'There's a place down by the river which should be empty at this time of year.'

'On one condition,' Anne said. 'It's on me.'

'Don't be—'

'Stop the car please. Hilly and I will walk back to Kingstown.'

He laughed. 'All right, if you insist.'

He drove down to a pub on the Wye and they took a table in one of the bow windows that looked out at the great river winding slowly past.

He fetched drinks and picked up menus and directed their attention to the blackboard. 'They do a good steak-and-kidney pie,' he said. 'Make it themselves.'

'That'll do me,' Anne said. 'Hilly?'

'Can I have a starter and a pudding?'

The pub was almost empty and when they had finished their lunch Hilly asked if she could take Beanie down to the river.

'You're lucky,' Tom said, as they watched the small girl and the tiny dog run along the bank.

'You've said that before and I'm touching wood again. You never thought of having a child?'

'I did, but Stephanie said there were things she wanted to do first.'

'Such as?'

'Sleep around, I imagine, because that's what she did.'

'Sorry, I didn't mean it that way, what I meant—'

'I know what you meant. Let's skip it.'

The tension was back as Anne had suspected it would be. She had been away with Tom before, to medical conferences, but that was business; this was personal.

She liked to think she had come because it would be better for Watch and her father to pick up the pieces of their relationship by themselves and not to have her and Hilly getting in the way.

Okay?

And she needed a break herself.

Okay?

Why was she getting like this? Who the hell did she have to explain things to anyway?

She realised he was looking at her expectantly. She'd missed what he'd said. 'Sorry?'

'I was saying that Roger is getting nervous. I think he's worried that you're involved in the Chitty case.'

'That's because I was involved with Jameson.'

'It's more than that. I suspect he's not sure of himself with women.'

'I suppose that's natural, given that he's the governor of an all-male prison.' She stirred her coffee, then said, 'Tom, I went to see the Chittys when you were in London.'

'Any joy?'

'The word joy doesn't drop naturally from the mouth when talking about them. No, they chased me away, but then something happened which is curious and interesting.'

She told him about bumping into Kenny on his imaginary motorbike and emphasised how hard she had tried to have him physically examined.

'And you say his mother said forget it?'

'She said he bumped into things all the time and she would cope.'

'That's odd, it's usually the other way round. As in: "You injured my boy, where's the money?"'

'I know, but it got odder. I was asking her if she thought Mason could have killed Sandra Benson and she said if you began life as a girl then became a boy you'd be capable of anything. What's that supposed to mean?'

He frowned. 'Could be she meant that Mason had been effeminate as a child. People in a village know a hell of a lot about each other. He's not married, is he?'

'No, but that doesn't signify. He says he was having an affair with Sandra, don't forget.'

'Youths sometimes go through gay phases. He might have been bisexual. Did she expand on that?'

'No. When I wanted her to she started ironing and then Kenny came in. He'd been digging and she made him go and wash again so I left and went to the shop. I was going to ask about the TV documentary but it was full of customers. I'll go back another time.'

'Talking about TV, I got hold of the manager at Kingstown General and he says that so far he knows there wasn't a call from any TV reporter to find out about Mason Chitty. The only calls were from his brother and his sister.'

'His brother and who?'

'His sister. Lives up north somewhere.'

'Tom, he hasn't got a sister.'

126

'Aah.' He was silent for a moment and then said, 'Sophie Lennox?'

'Could be.'

'Could also be a woman reporter from any of the tabloids or the local papers.'

'Would the hospital have mentioned paracetamol?'

'Not even to nearest family at that stage.'

Hilly came in, carrying Beanie.

'Don't worry about it,' Tom said. 'Enjoy your weekend.'

They left the pub and went on up the Wye valley.

Henry and Watch were in Henry's sitting-room surrounded by African artefacts. Some, like the Ndebele beadwork and the Saan Bushmen bows and arrows, were hanging on the walls, others like Zulu assegais and Pondo beer strainers were piled on the floor still awaiting their permanent homes. Between the two men was a bottle of brandy on a carved Ovambo stool.

Henry had not thought of Watch as a heavy drinker until he had seen him dispatch two brandies at the Mayfly. Many years before, in his cups, Watch had got into a fight in a bar in Maseru. The bar owner had wanted to prosecute him but Henry had been soothing, and money had changed hands. The whole incident was soon forgotten by everyone but Watch, who was deeply ashamed and swore off intoxicating liquor.

Now the long drought, it seemed, was over, and fuelled by brandy which he drank as Southern Africans do, with water, he was talking.

'He cooks where?' Henry said.

'The hotel at TY.'

Henry remembered the small and pretty hotel at Teyateyaneng. 'So what you're saying is this cook . . . what'shisname . . . Julius—?'

'Junius.'

'Junius. What you're saying is he only worked part week, is that right?'

'The weekends, Judge.'

'And the rest of the week, the greater portion, he was at your sister's house in Maseru?'

Henry's questioning had unwittingly taken on the flavour of the courtroom and Watch, who had heard as much of this as any man alive, reacted to it in a formal way even though the whites of his eyes, more a dusky yellow, were now showing red flecks after the drinks.

He said, 'He was wekkin' all weekends from breakfast on Saturday morning to dinner on Sunday night.'

'He wasn't the proper cook, then?'

'He was the second cook.'

'Right. So from Mondays he was with you, or perhaps I should say your sister. How old is she by the way?'

'Fifty-two. Too old for that eh-kind of thing, Judge. She got children from her marriage. She got one at the university and one who wants to go.'

'And she's got Junius. Have another.'

He poured Watch another brandy. 'I take it you don't get on with him.'

'He a rogue, Judge. He takin' all the money in the house.'

'He sounds like a real twister.'

'That is him, a twister.'

'And that's why you left?'

'He takin' all my clothes and he takin' my pension. He standing at the post office because he knows what day the money comin' in.'

'Is that why you were throwing the bones? To damage him from this distance?'

Watch looked down at the brandy and swirled it round and round.

'Is it, Watch?'

'No, Judge.'

'Well, are you going to tell me?'

Watch sat motionless.

'Listen, old man, you may be the greatest witch-doctor Lesotho has ever seen but I've known you for forty years and if you are it's a complete surprise to me.'

'I bought them when that damn cook came.'

'So you did intend to use them against him? Use their magic, I mean.'

'He was takin' my clothes and—'

'Yes, yes, but what's that got to do with now? With the woman at the pub?'

Watch looked him sharply. 'How you know that?'

'I know everything.' Henry said mysteriously. 'But I want you to tell me.'

Watch hung his head for a moment and then looked up. 'Watchman smell her, Judge.'

'What's that supposed to mean? Smell what?'

'Watchman smell . . .' he began circling his hand in the air. 'Watchman smell many things.'

Henry realised that Watch had slipped into the third person but his own whisky intake made him insensitive. 'Oh, come on, Watch, none of that now. I know who the woman is. And you probably do too. You've been reading the papers.'

'No, Judge, I haven't. I smell it.'

Henry registered the first person once again and smiled to himself. 'Smell what?'

'When the woman touches me. I smell death.'

'You old bugger, you could never smell death in Africa. At least you never told me you could.'

'I was born on Thaba Bosio. Born there on the mountainside. It is our mountain, Judge. Sacred . . .'

'All I know is that the British Army was badly mauled on those slopes in the last century. Oh, and Anne and I used to fly kites on it.'

Watch waved away these irrelevancies. 'My father could smell death. Now I smell death.'

'Whose death?'

'Someone belonging to that woman.'

Henry scratched his bald head. 'You never told me about all this.'

'Judge, I only found out when I bought the bones to ask them about the cook.'

'And what did they tell you?'

Watch said sadly, 'Nothing. But now they telling me about the woman.'

'Let's have a look at these bones of yours.'

Watch went to his room and came back with five small yellow vertebrae. They were smooth and worn by constant use.

'They look like human bones all right,' Henry said. 'Where did you get them?'

'I bought them in Maseru.'

'All right, show me what you do.'

Watch took the bones. His hand was shaking but he threw them on the carpet and studied them.

'What are they telling you?'

'They telling me nothing now, Judge.'

'What did they tell you before? When you were throwing them in your room.'

'They tell Watchman about the woman, Judge. Her son is dead.'

'Not her son, her daughter.'

'Her child.'

'And she's not only dead but she's been murdered and no one knows where the hell she is.'

'Maybe . . .'

'Maybe what?'

'Maybe I could find her?'

'Have another brandy, old chap, and don't talk nonsense.'

'It's not eh-nonsense.'

'Well, where is she then?' Henry was beginning to feel his own drinks.

'I think . . . maybe not too far away from the pub.'

Henry, who had been finding Watch's theatrical impression of a witch-doctor diverting, looked at him with more interest and finally said, 'All right. If you're so bloody clever why don't we have a look round there sometime.'

Lily watched the Admiral at the bar. Being Saturday evening the Mayfly was crowded and the Admiral was not a big man. But the moment he reached the counter the barman swiftly moved to serve him. There were one or two black looks from other waiting customers but nothing was said. He's upper class, Lily thought, that's why. The conclusion might have caused a mixture of anger and envy in others, but she admired his self-confidence.

She had dressed for him in a simple, fitted black crepe dress which flattered her neat waist and flared out below the hips. She had contemplated adding a *diamanté* brooch and matching ear-rings Barry had given her but, wondering uneasily whether the Admiral might find them vulgar, had finally settled for a single row of pearls which she thought looked almost real against the black. She had taken more time with her make-up than she had for years and when he picked her up he had said, 'You're looking very good, Lily.' She had forgotten how nice it was to receive a compliment.

He came back with her gin and tonic. She usually ordered a stout or a cider. But she knew instinctively that those were not the sort of drinks she should order when she was with Sir Peter.

'Cheers,' he said. He dabbed his lips with a red-and-white polka-dotted handkerchief. 'Not a bad week. Not a good week but not bad. We've achieved some sort of results. I know you'd think them negative but just to know where she *isn't* is a positive step.'

'I think so too,' she said.

They had been out searching twice now and Sandra's best friend, Betty Sugden, still had to join them. It wasn't surprising, she had always been undependable. Lily couldn't say she enjoyed the searches but she was getting used to them. She'd worn trousers and had bought herself a pair of proper outdoor shoes so she had been able to cope better with the rough ground. The Admiral had phoned her only an hour before suggesting they meet at the pub because he wanted to tell her the results of the other working parties. Or, more accurately, the fact that the other parties had reported no results either. That's what he was explaining now, about negatives and positives, and as he talked, her faith in him increased and she found herself becoming more optimistic that they would eventually find Sandra.

As she was finishing her gin and tonic she decided to ask him back to her house for a meal, but when she had mentally gone through what she had in the fridge, she changed her mind.

And then he said, 'I'm hungry, aren't you? I've left it rather late but if you're not doing anything else, would you join me for dinner in the grill room?'

She smiled and said, 'You know, Sir Peter, I was just thinking—'

'And I'd be grateful if you'd call me Peter. The handle sounds so formal. Should I go and see about a table?'

'That would be lovely.'

It was while he was standing at the restaurant door, that she saw she was being studied by two men. One of them was black and she didn't like the look of him at all.

14

'You've got good bones,' Fanny Fielder said, touching Hilly on the cheek. 'Lovely things, bones.'

Tom said, 'Watch out, Hilly, mother will want you to sit for her.'

'Not this weekend,' Tom's mother said. 'This is a holiday for us all.' She turned to Anne. 'How's your drink?'

'I'm fine, thank you.'

'Please, darling.' She handed Tom her glass. He went over to the drinks cabinet and poured her a gin. It was a Jonge Jenever from Holland and the bottle sat in an ice bucket. It was pale yellow and she drank it neat out of a small shot glass.

Fanny Fielder was a large and handsome woman and she lived in a large and handsome house which looked over the Wye to the Black Mountains beyond.

In many ways, Anne thought Tom's mother was like the house. Even now in her seventies she was still good-looking, but decay had set in around her neck and on the backs of her hands. She was wearing a red-and-yellow Moroccan caftan and lay back on a *chaise longue*.

She started a conversation with Tom about his

135

brother who had emigrated to Australia: had he heard from him? What was the news?

Anne let her thoughts wander back to their arrival that afternoon. Kilvert was a small village about five miles downstream from Hay on Wye. It lay on either side of a road bridge and Tom had turned off the road onto a track. Rain had started to fall.

The slippery track wound along the river bank and slowly the house had come into view: a glimpse of a window, part of the roof, a stone staircase. Then abruptly they had emerged from the trees and there it was, a lovely Italianate villa built of brick and yellow stone.

'It's gorgeous,' Anne had said.

'Pretty neglected, but Mother can't do much in the garden now, she's got a hip.'

Tom's mother did not meet them. 'We'll see her later,' he said as he showed them to their rooms.

Rain was dripping from the ceiling of Anne's room. Tom said, 'I'll get something.' He put a bucket underneath it. 'This used to be my room. I should have had it fixed but I don't get here much.' The room was cold and the steady drip of water did nothing to cheer Anne up.

They met Fanny Fielder when she came down for a drink before dinner. That had been about seven o'clock. It was now nearly nine and Tom said to his mother, 'Have you got anything in the house?'

'Like what, darling?'

'Like food. We're all starving.'

'Of course. There's God knows how much in the freezer.'

They left her watching the TV news and went into the kitchen. It was vast. There was a huge Aga cooker that wasn't on, and a fridge and freezer that were big enough to service a restaurant. There was also one of the biggest scrubbed-pine tables Anne had seen.

Tom looked in both the fridge and the freezer and then shrugged. 'How does bacon and eggs sound?'

'It sounds great,' Anne said. 'But let me—'

'Absolutely verboten. Or else you start the long walk back to Kingstown. Now, how do you like your bacon, Hilly, crisp or soggy?'

After supper Anne took Hilly to her room, which was next to her own. 'Are you going to be all right here?' she said.

'I haven't had a bath.'

'We'll organise that tomorrow. You're not really dirty.'

Anne read her a story, then, when she fell asleep, went back to the drawing-room.

'Tom's making some calls,' Fanny said. 'If I was a better hostess I'd have got supper for you. Sorry about that.'

'We've had a lovely supper. Tom says you've got an arthritic hip, why don't you have a replacement?'

'Did he tell you to try to convince me? Well, I'll

tell you, men don't care much for women on crutches.' She paused, then added, 'Roberto was coming for the weekend but he can't get away.'

Roberto, Anne knew from Tom, was the latest in a line of younger lovers who came to stay with Fanny.

'That reminds me . . . Stephanie phoned,' Fanny said.

'Tom's ex-wife?'

'I meant to tell him. She wanted to come this weekend. I said no. I wish she'd just accept that she's no longer married to him. I really don't want to continue the relationship. But she phones me and wants to talk about Tom. I never liked her much.'

Anne did not want to discuss Stephanie and said, 'Can I get you another drink?'

'No, I've had enough for tonight. I'll sleep now.' She began to lever herself off the daybed.

'Let me help you.'

Fanny shook her head. 'When I start accepting help, I've had it.' She held onto chairs for balance. 'Good-night, my dear, sleep well.' Holding herself erect she walked from the room as though nothing was the matter.

Anne wondered if Tom had gone to bed. She waited for nearly ten minutes, then thought, to hell with this family. She switched off the lights and went upstairs and checked on Hilly. Then she washed, cleaned her teeth, and was getting into bed when there was a soft knock on the door. She slipped on a dressing-gown. 'Yes?'

'It's me,' Tom said. She opened the door. 'I'm sorry I was so long but I talked to Holroyd and a couple of other people.'

'Come in. I was just getting to bed.'

'It all took much longer than I expected, but it's been interesting. Look, wouldn't you like a nightcap?'

'I've just done my teeth . . . God, what a stupid thing to say. I can always do them again. Yes, please.'

She got into bed and Tom came back a few minutes later with a bottle of malt whisky. He gave her a glass and sat at the end of the bed.

'How's Hilly?' he asked.

'She's fine but we'd better keep our voices down.'

'Holroyd's found out what we rather suspected, that Sophie Lennox isn't working for anyone but is clearly trying to set up something on her own.'

'And she called the hospital pretending Mason was her brother?'

'I would think so. I phoned someone I know who's a sister at the Kingstown General, and she said she'd try to find out more. But then she mentioned Mason Chitty. She's interested in the case for another reason: her mother was the district nurse in the Stepton area when he was born.'

'Did you ask her about the sex change?'

'No, I didn't, but it's something you might ask

her mother. I got her address for you.'

'The Chittys get stranger by the day. The three of them all speak with different accents and use language in different ways. Mason's educated and speaks rather well but his brother Samuel had a broad Sussex accent and sounds less educated. His mother, on the other hand, doesn't sound like either of them.'

Tom said, 'I'm going to see if I can find Sophie Lennox. I want to have a word with her.'

'Will that do any good?'

'Maybe. I think it's worth a try.'

'I still feel bad about all this. If it wasn't for Jameson—'

'Don't. It'll work out. Another drop?'

'No thanks.' She handed him her glass and as she did so he put his fingers round her wrist.

She had been half expecting this. If you let a man into your bedroom late at night with a bottle of whisky in his hand there was no way you could tell yourself later that what happened next was all an enormous surprise. So far she had been determined that what was about to happen must never happen. Now a voice inside her said: why not?

There was an answer to that and it went like this: he's your boss; never sleep with your boss. But the voice said, not here he isn't. This is limboland. No one's a boss here.

He leaned forward and kissed her. The kiss wore

its intention on its sleeve. She kissed him back. And that wasn't any good-night kiss either. He slid onto the bed next to her and put his arms around her. She hadn't been held in this way since muscular Clive's time . . . And her body wanted what Tom wanted. Yes, she thought, this was limboland and what the hell!

The phone on the bedside table seemed to ring stridently inside her head. It rang again and she thought: Hilly!

She said, 'Answer it.'

He leant over and picked up the receiver. 'Yes?'

'Tom is that you? You are in your old room?'

The voice was plain for Anne to hear.

Tom swung his legs from the bed. 'What do you want?'

'What do I . . . Tom, have you got someone there?'

The voice was loud and Stephanie's French accent was clearly audible. Tom got up and cradled the phone close to his body, turning his back on Anne as though closing himself away in a different space.

He said, 'Listen, I—'

That was all Anne heard for Hilly's voice from the adjoining room called, 'Mummy!'

Tom half turned, but Anne flung back the bedclothes. 'Coming, darling.' She padded across to Hilly's door.

'I heard ringing,' Hilly said sleepily.

'It was the phone,' Anne sat on her bed. 'It was for Tom so I called him.'

'That used to be his room.'

'That's right.'

'Who is it?'

'I don't know, sweetie. Lie down and go to sleep.'

'Can I have Beanie?'

'No, darling.'

'Please.'

'Not tonight.'

'Please.'

'Oh, all right, I'll ask Tom.'

But when she went back into her own bedroom the telephone was on its cradle and Tom had gone.

'If this is supposed to be a gallop, I don't think much of it,' Henry said to Watch. 'You couldn't gallop a donkey up here.'

The two of them were standing just below the Chittys' gates.

'The man said we must go left, Judge,' Watch said.

They moved along the track that led down towards the river. A high wind was blowing out of the south-west and the Downs were covered in mist.

'What do your bones say now?' Henry asked.

'The bones don't speak. You know that, Judge.'

'Oh, come on Watch, lighten up a bit.'

Watch looked suddenly cross. 'You making fun of Watchman. He don't appreciate that.'

'All right . . . all right . . . but let's get on with it. It's going to start raining in a little while and we can't see much in this bloody mist.'

They turned away from the gates onto the track that led down to the river levels and the trees. Both men had sticks and were dressed for the weather. Watch was wearing his purple-and-gold top as a windbreaker over his ordinary clothing. Henry had made a note on the memo pad in Anne's kitchen to remind himself to buy him a plain-coloured anorak but he had not tried to dissuade him from wearing it in the meantime because Watch was beginning to show signs of his real self. His tiredness seemed to have gone.

'This is what the pub-keeper must have been referring to,' Henry said. 'We've now got the river on our left and the trees to our right. And look . . . there are some of the tapes he said we'd find.' He pointed to the red tapes which formed long alleys and were fluttering in the wind.

They came down to the wide, flat fields. 'God Almighty,' he said. 'If she's here it'll take a bloody army to find her.'

'She is here, Judge. I can eh-feel her.'

'Well, that's something.'

Watch looked at him again with irritation. He knew the Judge's tone of voice like he knew his own. And he told himself it wasn't his fault they were here. That was the fault, if not of the bones, then of the publican of the Mayfly. They had questioned him the evening before and he had been only too happy to tell them about the most notorious event that had happened to the village in living memory and the search for Sandra's body.

A group of people were coming along the river bank in the opposite direction and Henry said, 'Bloody tourists come to gawp, I suppose.'

They spent an hour or more on the bank looking down into holes and eddies and criss-crossing the field. The heavy mist turned heavier until it was unmistakably less of a mist than a drizzle. Every few minutes Henry would ask Watch if he had any more positive feelings about where the body might be but Watch just shrugged.

Finally Henry said, 'I'm getting soaked. I think we should pack it in.'

Watch shook his head.

Henry said, 'We can always come back another day.'

'If you don't want to look, Judge, you go back to the car.' And with that Watch walked, with his long mountain stride, towards the trees.

'Well, damn it all, I will,' Henry said.

He stood with his hands on his hips watching his former legal clerk, resplendent in gold and purple, disappear into the gloomy stand of trees that seemed to flow off the flat plain into the side of the Downs.

'Watch!' Henry called after him. 'Don't be a bloody fool, you'll catch your death if you go on like this.'

But Watch did not alter his stride pattern and

Henry said, 'Oh to hell with it!' and began to walk back to the car, which was parked just below the gallops.

He had got halfway there and was near the Chittys' gates once more when he slowed down and stopped. He couldn't really leave Watch by himself. So he walked to the river levels again, then turned into the trees. His feet made no noise for the leaf mould from the hardwoods was thick on the ground. He had to move around the roots of several huge trees uprooted by storms.

'Watch!' he shouted. A couple of pigeons, feeding on barley from one of the leaking black plastic bales that still littered the landscape from a previous harvest, burst upwards into flight and scared the life out of him.

'Watch! Where are you?'

A hen pheasant flew up onto the fallen trunk of a tree and stared at him in surprise before giving its fright call and flying off.

'Watch!'

He thought he heard a sound coming from a stand of small silver birch trees away to his left. 'Are you there? Have you found something?'

He walked towards the trees and the sound came again. This time it was a muffled call.

'Right, I'm coming. What have you got?'

He pushed into the dense thicket and the first thing he saw was the purple-and-gold tracksuit top. It lay on the ground. Watch lay inside it. He repeated the muffled sound Henry had heard.

'I'm here, old man! I'm right here!' Henry said, fearing he might have had a heart attack.

He knelt down, turned Watch over onto his side and saw that it was not a heart attack. His face was covered in blood and his nose was bleeding freely.

'Oh, Lord,' Henry said. 'Did you bump into something?'

Watch began to struggle to his feet and Henry helped him up.

'Did you trip? Is that what happened?'

Watch shook his head slowly. Then he felt his front teeth. They seemed intact. He said, 'A man hit me with a stick.'

'What?'

'A man.'

'What man?'

'A man. I don't know what man. He was behind a tree.' The blood was pouring from Watch's nose.

'Take my handkerchief,' Henry said. 'Let's get back to the car. Can you manage?'

He put his arm around Watch's waist and they began to walk.

'Didn't you see anything at all?'

Watch tried to speak but blood ran into his mouth.

'All right, don't say anything. Have you a hankie?'

Watch pulled one from his pocket. Henry's own

handkerchief was soaked with blood and he threw it away.

They went up the path along the face of the Downs. Watch muttered incoherently and Henry said, 'Don't try to talk. I was going to get you to the car but I think we should go to one of the houses and we can ring Anne. She should be back by now. Let's try that one over there.'

They walked down to Elizabeth Drayton's house and Henry banged on the door.

She has forgotten the gloves. No matter. Sandra is all around her. She sits on the hard brown kitchen chair in the pastel-coloured room that had belonged ... no, not had, did, belong to her daughter ... wherever she was ...

Sunday night, my love, she says to the room in general but to her daughter's photograph in particular. Do you remember how we used to go to church when Daddy was alive?

Not every Sunday, but often enough. Barry had said that in the Navy you went to church every Sunday even on board ship and he would have missed it. Sandra had never liked it much so once Barry wasn't there they had almost stopped except for Christmas, Easter and the harvest service. They'd gone the year before to harvest festival and that was the last time. Sandra had disappeared soon after that.

My love, I still think 'disappear'. Maybe I

*shouldn't but I have hope. And if that goes . . . well,
I shall mourn. That's what we need, the ability to
mourn. And to know. That's the worst part, the not
knowing. People go mad from not knowing.*

*I won't talk about that any more. I don't want to
talk about madness. I shouldn't be talking to you
like this.*

*But the Admiral says we will find you. The
working parties will go over every inch of ground.
He told me at dinner last night. He had a Dover
sole, ever so expensive, and I had what you always
liked best: Chicken Kiev. And we drank wine just
like we used to when Daddy took us out. I had white
and so did he. Two glasses for me and he drank
the rest of the bottle. And after dinner he walked
me home.*

*She realises, with a start, that this had happened
the previous night and she had not told Sandra
about it and she speaks hastily about the light rain
that had been falling when they came out.*

*Oh, yes, the weather has certainly changed these
last few days. The Admiral says there is a big
weather front coming in from Ireland so we must
dress warmly when next we go out.*

*I didn't ask him in though I think he would have
liked to come . . . But I hadn't cleaned the kitchen
properly, nor the sitting-room . . . I wanted to polish
the glasses. Can't serve drinks in smudgy glasses.
So I said thank you very much Peter . . . that's what
he's asked me to call him and it seems so silly going*

on calling him Sir Peter . . . so I said he must call
me Lily . . . We've said this before to each other but
somehow I couldn't . . . and then he couldn't because
I couldn't . . . but now we can . . . And when we were
at the Mayfly there was a black man looking at me
and this afternoon one of the other working parties
saw two men walking along the river and one of
them was a black man . . . I wonder if he's the
same . . . We don't have black men here very often . . .

She pauses.

Who is she talking to?

Sandra?

Or herself?

15

Limboland was far away, or so it seemed to Anne. The Land-Rover had turned off the motorway and was approaching Kingstown and she wasn't sure whether she was glad or sorry. Was a combination of her father and Watch better or worse than a combination of Fanny Fielder and telephones that rang in the night?

She wasn't sure about something else: whether she was pleased or sorry now that the telephone had rung. There was the usual tension between herself and Tom and she knew there would have been as much – or more – if the telephone hadn't rung. But at least she would have had . . .

What? Pleasure? Felt wanted? A requitement of lust?

As it was, Hilly had woken again and so she had ended up by taking her small daughter into bed with her instead of the large man.

What was bothering her now was whether what had happened would change the scenario of her life *vis-à-vis* Tom. She thought it might but by how much would depend on her. And Tom, of course. He had given an indication of how he was going to play things that morning.

Breakfast had been a scratch meal of cornflakes and toast and – this was nice – really good coffee. Then they had gone for a walk; Tom and Hilly and Beanie and herself. They had walked along the bank of the Wye for a couple of miles. For most of that time Hilly and Beanie had been well in front of them so they had had some moments of privacy.

'There's no point in pretending nothing happened.' Tom had said, 'and I just want to say how sorry I am that I . . . let me phrase that again . . . how sorry I am that things went wrong. There, I've said my little piece.' He took her hand and held it for a moment and went on. 'And I'm sorriest of all that what was about to happen didn't happen . . . and I hope you are too.'

'Yes, I am, I think.'

'And do you think it might?'

'What?'

'Happen again? No . . . I don't mean that do I? Because what was meant didn't happen. God, I'm getting tied up in clauses. But you know what I mean?'

'I thought that things had cooled between you and Stephanie.'

'They're like ice. At least on my side, but that doesn't stop her. I'm just pleased she didn't get you on the telephone.'

She thought: so am I. She remembered very well the last time she had met Tom's ex-wife a few months ago. The phone in her office had rung and the gatelodge had told her Stephanie was there, wanting to see her. At first she had said it must be a mistake, that Stephanie would have come to see Tom. But she had been assured that wasn't the case. So she had gone out.

She had met Stephanie only once before but recognised her instantly. She was standing in the bus shelter. Anne had been struck by how elegant she looked. She was short and slender with long, black, crimped hair and was dressed in black and white: black trousers, a white polo-neck sweater and a black trench coat flung casually over her shoulders. In the grey light her face had looked drawn, almost haggard.

'How can I help you?' Anne had said.

There were deep shadows under Stephanie's eyes, but the eyes themselves blazed like an animal's. She was smoking a cigarette and now ground it under a stiletto-heeled pump.

'Why are you doing this?' she had burst out.

'Doing what?'

'Don't pretend! You know what I mean.'

In the car now with Tom and Hilly Anne could remember the scene so well she could even hear Stephanie's French accent.

She had suddenly shouted, 'Do you think I do not know what is going on?'

'Is there something going on?'

'Between you and Tom.'

'I'm afraid you've made a mistake.'

'Don't lie to me. I know. You think you can hide behind a child? You think I don't know what it is?'

Anne had tried to cut the conversation short at this point but Stephanie had said, 'Tom is no good for you. He can never love someone like you. This is a warning, you understand, next time things will be different.'

Well, so far there hadn't been a next time, for which Anne was profoundly grateful.

As they walked along the Wye and watched Hilly run with Beanie, Tom had said, 'She talked for half an hour. I knew she would, that's why I went to my room. I couldn't come back after that.'

'You'd have found two of us in bed. Hilly couldn't sleep. I suppose I shouldn't ask about Stephanie but is there nothing you can do? I'm assuming you want to do something.'

'Very much. But what? She's been coming up here, Mother says. Trying to work herself back into the family I suppose.'

'I thought she had someone else.'

'Oh, yes. A merchant banker. They were married briefly.' He walked in silence for a while, then said, 'I might have guessed something like this would happen. She was so febrile. Her father was everything to her. He was an ENT consultant in one of the big Paris hospitals and after her mother died he brought her up. They had a boat and a holiday home at Port Grimaud and, of course, a big apartment near the Bois in Paris. Then he died

and she started working for a charity. I met her
when I went out to the Sudan with one of the
British medical teams during the famine in the mid-
Eighties. When I came back to England she came
with me and we got married. I think she simply
wanted me as the replacement father figure.
Someone she could come home to when she had
tired of her latest bed companion.'

'Was it bad?'

'From time to time.'

'Sorry, I shouldn't be prying.'

'Oh, what the hell, it makes no difference now.'

Kingstown hove into sight in a thin drizzle. The
prison on the skyline gave it a sinister look in the
gloaming. But the house was welcoming and even
more so because her father and Watch were not
there.

She offered Tom a drink and was about to pour
it when Hilly came jumping down the stairs.
'There's a message on the machine! Can I work it?'

'Hang on,' Anne said. 'I'll come with you. You
never take down phone numbers.'

She went up with Hilly and turned on the
machine. Her father's voice said, 'It's now ten to
six. Watch has had an accident. He seems better
but I'd like you to see him before we try to get him
home. You said you'd be back about six, that's why
I'm phoning. We're at Mrs Drayton's house in
Stepton.' He gave her directions and a phone
number.

155

She phoned but the line was engaged so she went down to Tom and explained.

He said, 'If it's not my telephone, it's yours.'

Lily had cleaned Sandra's room twice that Sunday as a form of penance for not telling Sandra immediately about her dinner with Sir Peter. Odd how she still thought of him as Sir Peter yet was now able to call him Peter. It was the same kind of hang-up she had had calling Mrs Drayton Elizabeth. She finished vacuuming and dusting and then cleaned the mirrors and the glass on the photographs and decided she would also do the windows. But when she looked the afternoon was dark and had turned to drizzle, so that wasn't possible. Still, there were lots of other things she could clean and she was on her way downstairs when the doorbell rang. It would be Peter, she thought, come to talk about arrangements for their working party and to give her the new lists of times for the coming week.

But it wasn't. She found Mitchell standing on the step. She half closed the door so as to be ready to slam it if need be and he said, 'I got something to say to you.'

'What is it?'

'I don't like to talk here.'

'I meant what's it about?'

'What d'you think it's about.'

'Sandra?'

'I can find her.'

156

'What?'

'You want me to talk about it here?'

'No . . . I . . . You'd better come in.'

On the doorstep he had just been a dark shape against the gloomy sky. Now he came into the lighted sitting-room and his face was darker than most people's and his long black hair glistened. He smelled strongly of the stables.

In his hand he held a package wrapped in dusty black plastic. 'I can find her with this,' he said.

He put it down on the table and began to unwrap it. 'Not here,' she said. 'Come into the kitchen.'

She wasn't sure what she was expecting, but whatever she had expected, it wasn't a couple of sticks. Then she saw that there weren't two sticks but one and they formed a large letter Y.

'Dowsin' stick,' he said.

'A what?'

'Ain't you ever heard of dowsin'?'

'Never.'

'Divinin' then? Water divinin'?'

'Mr Mitchell, I think you'd better wrap up your—'

'Hang on a sec. You ain't hear of water divinin'?'

'No.'

'How'd you think they found water . . . I means in the old days? They found it with this. Those that could do it. It ain't everyone. Oh, no. It's special. I'm a dowser. Got it from my father who got it from his. I can find water.'

'I don't want water.'

'I knows that. But I'm just saying. And not only water. Metal too. I found a buried box once with old-fashioned tools in it. Up by Blackdown before Mrs Drayton sold it to the Chittys.'

'We're not looking for metal either, Mr Mitchell.'

'I knows that too, but she could have been wearing metal. Rings. Necklaces. Things like that. Was she?'

'I suppose so. Yes. Of course. She always wore rings and brooches. She wore a lot of jewellery.'

'And that don't rot.'

She flinched and he said, 'Excuse me but it's the truth. You got to get used to it. I mean, what if we finds her? We ain't going to find her lookin' like she was going up to London for the day.'

'Stop it!'

'But you got to understand it and you got to face it. You started something and you got to know what's at the end of the road.'

'Leave it . . . leave it . . . !'

'That's for you to say. I can leave it or I can find her. Up to you.'

Lily had buried thoughts of what Sandra might look like now deep down in her mind, so deep that she never examined them nor ever spoke about them. And neither Peter nor anyone else had ever mentioned such a thing. Sandra was Sandra, a beautiful young girl who was . . .

What? . . . Where? . . .

She had been able not to consider the answers and now this horrible Mitchell had—

'Look.' He fished a small woman's handkerchief from his pocket. 'Is that hers?'

'What d'you mean . . . ? Oh, my God! Sandra's? Where did you find it?'

He did not answer but held the handkerchief up for her to look at. She reached for it. He pulled it away and held it to his nose.

'There ain't no scent but then there wouldn't be after all these months, would there?'

'Where did you find it?' It was almost a shout.

Again he did not answer but passed her the handkerchief. It was stained with mud and what she took to be leaf mould. It was a simple white handkerchief of which she and Sandra must have had a dozen each. She looked at it in detail but it had no distinguishing marks on it for they did not send clothes to a laundry.

Tears came without her even knowing they were near. They flooded from her eyes and ran in rivulets down her cheeks.

'I didn't say it was hers,' Mitchell said. 'All I done was ask.'

She sat down at the kitchen table and held her apron up to her eyes. 'Please tell me . . . where did you find it?'

'It was down there. That's all I'm saying. But I can find her for you.'

She held the handkerchief to her nose and

breathed in. The smell, if there was one, was of horses, absorbed from the lining of Mitchell's pocket.

'Did you find it with that?' She indicated the dowsing stick.

'Lord no, you can't find things like that with dowsin' sticks. No, they got to be buried. Underground water. Metal. And bodies.'

'Because of the . . .'

He nodded. 'Because of the metal. Can't get no signal from bones.'

She flinched again. Here in her hand was something tangible, something that might have belonged to Sandra; the first thing associated with her that the working parties or anyone attached to them had found. Could he help? Could he find her?

He said, 'Come outside. Let me show you.' He rose and although she did not want to go with him she found herself following him into the back garden. It was not a very big garden but large hedges cut off the other houses. There were some shrubs and a single flower bed which Kenny had dug over for her and which was waiting for bedding plants.

He stood at one end of the oblong lawn and said, 'This is how you holds it, see?' He took the two Y ends, one in each hand, and held the stick, which was about three feet long, directly in front of him in a horizontal position. His hands did not grip the wood in the normal way but inside out, the palms each facing outwards.

'You got to know how she knocks,' he said. 'You walks like this.' He came towards her. 'Watch the tip.'

She watched the tip of the dowsing stick and when he was halfway down the lawn towards her she saw it dip down suddenly.

'See that?'

'Is that what it's supposed to do?'

'That was only me. I wants to show you how she dips. You can feel it in your hands like when you're fishin' and a fish takes the hook. Same sort of tug.' In the gloom he moved away from her and, still holding the dowsing stick in front of him, he began to go back along the lawn, then he moved to his right and started covering the newly dug flower bed. Lily shivered with chill, and with apprehension and unease. She was about to say they should go in when he called,' You see that?'

'See what?'

'She's talkin' to me. Oh, yes. Now, she's talkin' to me.'

Sandra? Here? In the garden? Oh, dear God!

'What you sayin', old girl? What you tellin' me?'

Lily, in horror, began to back away towards the kitchen door.

Mitchell was going forward in the flower bed now, his feet churning up the soil. 'Speak to me, my love. Tell me where it is.'

And then she realised he was talking not to her dead Sandra but to the dowsing stick.

Suddenly he dropped onto his knees and began to dig with his hands.

'What have you found?' she called.

He ignored her. Then he stopped digging and, with his back to her, reached down into the hole he had dug and held something up.

'You come and look at this,' he said.

She did not move.

'Come along. This won't hurt you none.'

'Is it Sandra's?' she said.

'Not this. No, never this.'

The drizzle was slanting down and hitting her in the face and she wished he had never come and that she was not standing with him in her garden.

'I'll come to you, then,' he said.

He approached her and she saw his boots were covered in mud. Whatever it was in his hand was also covered in wet soil and he was brushing it with his fingers.

'See? Metal.'

'What is it?'

'It's an old rim lock, that's what it is.'

He held it so she could see. It was certainly an old lock and much had been eaten away by rust.

'Where did it come from?' she said.

'Thrown away years ago. Long before you ever came here or this house was built. Just thrown down and forgotten and now . . . well, found again.'

He had tucked the dowsing stick under one arm and now he pulled it out and patted it. 'She knows,'

162

he said. 'She can find things.'

It was true, Lily thought. She *could* find things. And if she could—

Mitchell finished the thought for her. 'That's what she can find. Metal. And your Sandra was wearing metal. See? Shall I come inside and we can talk?'

She looked at his boots. 'We can talk here.'

He shrugged and stood on the lawn in the drizzle.

'Bring it next time we go out,' she said. 'Then we can all see.'

'This ain't for a working party. This ain't for people like the Admiral and that stupid Kenny. This is between you and me, the two of us.'

She didn't know what to say to that but she didn't want to lose the possibility of him finding something of Sandra – she couldn't think of him actually finding her daughter.

'I'd come out with you.' She was frightened at the very thought. 'I've got the time.'

'Time ... now that's the thing. I ain't got the time. Time's valuable.'

'You want payment?'

'She ain't my daughter.'

16

'Another drink, doctor?' Elizabeth Drayton said.

'No, thanks,' Anne said. 'I think we should be getting back. Hilly's got school tomorrow.'

'I'm not tired,' Hilly said.

'Oh, you can't go yet,' Elizabeth said. 'What about you, Judge Vernon? And Mr Malopo?'

'That's very kind of you,' Henry said. 'I must say when we came down that hill we couldn't have hoped for all this.'

No, Anne thought, nor could she. They were in the large drawing-room of Stepton House and if she had arrived without knowing the others she might have thought they were early guests at a drinks party. Watch, it was true, had been lying on his back on the sofa with a small towel under his nose but by the time she and Hilly arrived the bleeding had stopped and her services weren't needed.

'My son boxed when he was a young lad,' Elizabeth said. 'I got used to dealing with bloody noses. They all stop eventually.'

Henry said, 'Well, here's to you, Mrs Drayton, and our very sincere thanks for all you've done.'

'Nonsense. I'm grateful for the company. I was

supposed to go out to dinner last night but I wasn't feeling too well so meeting you all is a great pleasure. I'm just sorry Mr Malopo suffered as he has. It's not our usual way in Stepton though with what's been going on even places like this are not safe any longer.' She turned to Anne. 'When will the case resume?'

'Not for a week or so. I want Mason to be strong enough to endure several more days.'

'Can you tell us what happened when he fainted in the dock?'

'I'm afraid I can't,' Anne said.

Elizabeth turned to Henry. 'Are you going to report the attack on Mr Malopo?'

'Oh, yes. Can't have visitors to these shores being set upon like that.'

She said to Watch, 'And you never saw anyone?'

'Nothing.'

'Not even a figure?'

Watch hesitated.

'Go on,' Henry said. 'You said you thought it was someone hiding behind a tree.'

Still Watch hesitated.

'Did you?'

'Judge, I'm not sure. I was eh-lookin' down at the ground. And when I looked up something hit me in the face. I thought I saw a figure behind a tree but—'

'It could have been a branch in the wind,' Elizabeth said. 'It's very windy there. And if you looked up suddenly . . . I mean it could be, couldn't it?'

Watch was sitting up now and he nodded slowly. 'I cannot say for sure,' he said.

'I hope it was only a branch,' Elizabeth said. 'Anyway, it allowed me to meet you . . . and I hope you'd enjoyed your walk up till then.'

'It's a beautiful landscape,' Henry said.

'Yes, it is. One of my neighbours wanted to buy this land but I wouldn't sell. It's been in the family for generations.'

'They seemed to be surveying there,' Henry said. 'There were a great many tapes blowing in the wind.'

'I think they are telephone poles or something like that,' she said vaguely.

Anne stood up. 'Hilly and I must be off.' There was a general draining of glasses and expressions of thanks, then Henry and Watch went to Henry's car. Anne said her goodbyes and as she was about to get into her own car said to Elizabeth, 'You know the Chittys, of course.'

'Yes, I know them.' The tone was chilly.

'Could I come to talk to you about Mason? I'm worried about him.'

Elizabeth Drayton opened her mouth, closed it, then said, 'There's not much I can tell you.'

'Anything might help.'

'Am I allowed to? Isn't all this *sub judice*?'

'I'm responsible for him until he goes back for

167

trial and I want to be able to deliver him in good shape. There are one or two things I'd like to know that might make a difference.'

'I'll see. Ring me.'

Anne had to be satisfied with that.

'Psychics?' the Admiral said.

'Well, you know, those sorts of people,' Lily said.

They were in the sitting-room. She had phoned him when Mitchell left and he had come round in half an hour. There had been just time enough to run a vacuum cleaner over the floor and a duster over the furniture. She still thought the windows needed cleaning.

Peter was sitting in the chair Barry had bought because it supported his back, and he had a glass of whisky in his hand. He had poured it himself – she had asked him to get the drinks because she knew men liked that – and it looked much stronger than she would have poured.

As she went to her chair she caught a glimpse of herself in a mirror hanging over the fireplace. She was wearing a brown-and-green paisley dress that she used to keep for best. Her face seemed to have lost its haggard look and, for a change, she was quite pleased with what she saw.

'I don't really believe in psychics,' he said. 'I was a sub-lieutenant in the old *Portland* in the late Fifties or early Sixties – can't remember now – and we were on a visit to Rotterdam when that business

was going on with the Queen of the Netherlands.'
Lily looked blank. 'When it was said that a woman
psychic was trying to influence Queen Juliana. You
remember that, don't you?'

'I was at school then.'

He smiled. 'Yes, of course. Well, they had a hell
of a time with her and the whole country was up in
arms. Rather put me off psychics.' Then he said,
'Are you talking about magic? Soothsaying? ESP?
You know, I take a piece of your clothing or
something you've been using and hold it and
pretend to read your mind.'

'Gloves?'

'Anything.'

'No, not quite that.'

He was looking just right, she thought; just how
an English naval gentleman should look on a
Sunday evening in the country: green corduroy
trousers, an old tweed jacket, a checked shirt, and
a tie. Yes, a tie!

'What are you getting at, Lily?'

She took a sip of her fruit juice. 'Finding things.'

'Finding . . . ? Now hang on. You don't mean . . . ?
Yes, you do. You mean Sandra, don't you?'

'Someone came, you see.'

'Who came?'

'He said I wasn't to mention his name. I promised.'

That was a lie. She hadn't promise anything, but
standing there in the dark drizzle with Mitchell
holding the stick in his hands with the mud all

169

over his boots and the livid face and the piercing eyes and the talk of bones and him saying, 'This is just between ourselves. Understand me?' – with all that, fear was as good as a promise.

'Lily, you owe it to yourself.'

'I can't break a promise.'

'I suppose not. Not a promise. But you can tell me what he offered, can't you?'

'Oh, yes. He offered to find Sandra.'

'Christ Almighty! Sorry. Are you going to tell me how?'

'He had a stick.'

'He was going to find her with a stick, was he? That would be a wand, would it? A magic wand? He'd wave it and abracadabra there she'd be.'

'A dowsing stick, he called it.'

'Those things water diviners use?'

'He said they could find metal too. He found this in the garden.' She unwrapped the old lock and passed it to him.

'Where?'

'In the flower bed.'

'Lily . . . Lily . . .'

'It's true. I swear to God.'

He looked at the lock for a few moments and rubbed his fingers over the rusty parts. 'Did you see him find it?'

'I was in the garden. He was using the stick. He went over the flower bed forwards and backwards, left to right—'

170

'Yes, but did you see him actually find it?'

She tried to remember. 'He was standing with his back to me and then he crouched down and began digging. The stick had pointed downwards, you see.'

'Did you see the stick point downwards?'

'I don't think I actually saw it dip but it must've because he crouched down and started digging in the soil with his hands and soon he brought up the lock.'

'But you didn't see the stick dip or him actually bringing up the lock from the hole he'd dug?'

'What do you mean, Peter?'

'What I mean is that it would have been easy for him to drop the lock on the ground and pretend he'd found it. Any bloody fool can hold a dowsing stick in his hands and make it look like it's dipped.'

'I can't believe that.'

'Why not? You're standing some yards away, he's got his back to you blocking the view. It would have been simple. Tell me, is he doing all this out of the goodness of his heart?'

'He said it would take time.'

'And time was money?' She did not speak and he finally said, 'How much, Lily?'

'Two hundred pounds. He said it might take days, even weeks and he could only do it a couple of times a week because of his work.'

'Did you give him anything . . . any money?'

She shook her head. 'He wanted fifty pounds

down and I said it was Sunday night and I didn't have that much in the house and the banks wouldn't be open till tomorrow. That's why I phoned you. I wanted to get your advice. I mean you've done everything so far, all the working parties and things like that. Without you . . . well, there wouldn't be a search.'

'And are you glad or sorry?'

'About our search? Very glad.'

'Are you going to pay him?'

'Not if you think I shouldn't.'

'I can't say that to you, Lily. You're her mother.'

She stood up and took his glass. 'Another?'

He rose with her, put his hands on her shoulders and kissed her. For a moment she thought it was the kind of kiss she was used to these days: kisses for Christmas as she thought of them. But this wasn't. It came so unexpectedly and gave her such a jolt that she thought she was going to fall. She was holding his glass in one hand and with the other gripped the arm of a chair. He was a little taller than she was.

He put his hand on her breast.

'No,' she said.

'Why not?'

She tried to twist away from him but the backs of her knees were against the chair and she felt she might suddenly collapse into it. That would be embarrassing.

He kissed her again. She smelled smells she had

not smelled for a long time: whisky, rough tweed, sweat, Imperial Leather – masculine smells that burst into her brain.

Part of that brain was still functioning. 'I can't,' she said, trying to move his hand from her breast.

'Yes, you can.'

'Peter, I can't. Not here.'

'Yes, you can. Here.'

'Not with Sandra in the house.'

He began to unbutton her dress.

'Sandra isn't in the house.'

She felt his fingers. They were cool on her hot skin. God, what am I doing, she thought.

He touched her nipple and she jumped slightly.

He said, 'People think, when you're in your sixties, that it's all over. But it isn't, you know.'

'Peter, I don't think we should.'

'We're not hurting anyone, are we?'

She did not reply and his hand went into her bra and cupped her breast.

'Are we?' he repeated.

'I . . . No. We're not hurting anyone . . . I suppose . . .'

'Well, then . . .'

'Surveying tapes?' Anne said to her father. 'Telephone poles?'

They were by themselves in Anne's sitting-room. Henry said, 'Well, I had to pretend I didn't know what was going on. And then she pretended nothing

ALAN SCHOLEFIELD

was going on, didn't she?'

She smiled. 'I go away for a couple of days and come back to find you having a party with the local *grande dame*.'

'I wouldn't call it a party but she was good to Watch.'

'Do you think he was attacked?'

'I don't quite know what to believe. He said he had been, then he couldn't be sure. I'm wondering if he simply became embarrassed to find himself being looked after by a woman. Old Watch is pretty conservative. And there's the business behind the bones . . . oh, you don't know about the cook, do you, and why he bought the bones?'

He told her about Watch's unhappy experiences with his sister's boyfriend and she shook her head. 'Poor Watch.'

'That's what started him on all this second-sight business.'

'It doesn't seem to have done much good. The cook still got all his clothes and he hasn't achieved anything here.'

'What do you suggest; that I take the bones away from him?'

'You're the old Africa hand, I leave that to you. But one thing I do suggest and that is that you keep Watch out of this case. It's not his business and I have enough on my plate as it is. I wish to goodness I could get Mason back to court and have him proved innocent and then we could get rid of

174

the whole nasty mess – throwing bones and—'

'For heaven's sake, get that right. It's throwing *the* bones.'

'You know what I mean.'

'And while you're getting things right, there's something else. Mr Chitty will never be proved innocent. Under English law he can only be found not guilty and that doesn't mean he's innocent.'

'You should have been a lawyer,' Anne said.

The phone rang and an unfamiliar woman's voice identified herself as an agency nurse at the prison hospital.

Anne frowned. 'Where's Dr Naidoo?'

'I understand he was taken ill and I was called in.'

'Go on.'

'It's Mr Chitty. I feel unhappy about him. I know he's not on any medication but he was breathing so heavily I tried to wake him. He's sort of round now but his voice is slurred.'

'Okay. I'll come in but I want you to ring Security. Get a discipline officer and move him to the ward. Move him semi-prone and he'll co-operate. I'll be with you in twenty minutes. Oh – and nurse, warn Security to expect me.'

She drove quickly through the deserted Sunday-night streets of Kingstown, her mind focused on Mason Chitty. She knew only too well from Jameson the devastating effects on the brain of a sick liver which allowed digestive products to bypass its chemical processing and pour poison into the general circulation. And yet ... so soon after his overdose? Acute liver failure usually happened a bit later.

She parked the car, knocked on the familiar huge black gatehouse door and was quickly escorted by a night auxiliary through the strangely still prison.

Mason was in the ward, sitting up in bed. He was talking freely but tripping from word to word and what he was saying did not make much sense. She thought a word that kept coming up was 'tackling' but she could not fit it into a pattern. His loud and rambling talk had woken the other patients and one said, 'For Christ's sake, doc, tell him to shut up!'

'Do you know what he's saying?' she said.

The patient said, 'He's been on about his bloody food. Roast pork this and roast pork that! I'm bloody sick of it.'

Anne turned to the nurse. 'Can you check what he's had?'

She had clearly written that he was to have a protein-free diet until he was out of danger, but now the nurse came back and told her he'd had what the others had eaten: roast pork and crackling. She could hardly imagine anything worse.

She sat on Mason's bed and took his pulse. She had no interest in its rate for its own sake but the familiar manoeuvre gave her the opportunity she wanted to look closely at him. She watched for involuntary movements of his hands. They were steady enough. She chatted about trivia. He seemed to relax. She decided there was nothing so badly amiss that she need create organisational havoc by transferring him to Kingstown General at this hour on a Sunday evening.

She went to her room. The examination couch offered itself. She had used it before. It was going to be a long and uncomfortable night.

17

'They're going to kill me!'

'Who's going to kill you, Mr Monks?' Anne said.

'Them . . .' He waved his hands in the air to encompass the prison. He was middle-aged, thin-faced, with a full head of dark hair some of which had gone grey. His eyes were almost black and darted from side to side as he spoke. His teeth were dark brown and rotting.

'Have you been threatened?' she asked.

'All the time.'

'And have you reported it?'

'To the screws? They don't believe me.'

'It's their job to investigate threats to prisoners.'

He looked down at his hands, the fingers of which were yellow from cigarettes. 'They say good riddance.'

'I'm sure you've got that wrong.'

'They say anybody who interferes with a . . . with a . . .'

'Juvenile.'

'They say good riddance. And I never did it!'

'That's what you'll say at your trial then.'

'You don't believe me neither!'

'It's not my job to believe you or disbelieve you.

That's for the judge and—'

'Don't give me that shit. You're supposed to be on my side. You're supposed to be a medical person.'

'I'm not supposed to be on anybody's side. I'm just supposed to get you to court in good physical shape.'

'Like that Chitty bastard! You're on his side. Everyone in here knows it. They know how you talk to him; they know you think he didn't do it, well I'm telling you he did!'

'How do you know that, Mr Monks?'

'Because I know it. You think I don't? Well, I do. Yeah, he did it. He's the type. I seen pictures of him in the papers. Just the type. And I'm not.'

'You asked to see me and you're seeing me but I don't yet know what you want.'

'I want to sleep. I keep thinking they're coming in to kill me and I don't get no sleep. I want some valium.'

'Is that why you've come?'

'You gave Chitty valium in the hospital.'

'I don't discuss my patients.'

'I want some valium.'

'I'm sorry but I'm not prepared to—'

He rose and came towards her desk. 'You're just a bloody woman, you ain't got any right in a man's prison, you—'

She pressed a button under her desk top.

'Don't you fucking listen? I want some—'

Bells sounded. Feet crashed in the passageway.

The door was flung open by Les Foley. Behind him several prison officers came crowding into the room, one whipping off his glasses.

'Mr Monks is leaving now,' Anne said.

'Right you are,' Foley said. 'Let's be having you, Mr Monks.'

Monks looked as though he was going to make a fight of it and then the spirit drained out of him and he allowed himself to be shepherded away.

After Foley had removed Monks her room was suddenly quiet. Then she heard Tom's voice. She could catch occasional words but not sentences and she thought he sounded angry. She put her head round the door.

Les was back in his cubby-hole. 'Don't know what's come over the medical staff this morning,' he said.

She smiled at him. 'Thanks for being so prompt with Monks.' It was on the tip of her tongue to ask him what was happening in Tom's room, then she stopped herself. She liked Les as an assistant, not a gossip. She was turning back into her room when she saw Jenks come bustling out of Tom's room. He was flushed and his face looked angry but also apprehensive.

Her phone rang and she picked it up. It was Tom.

'You're in good voice this morning,' she said.

He did not react. 'Can you come in for a moment?' It was as though he was talking to a stranger. He was standing by the window and after a moment he said, 'You remember that film *I'm all right, Jack*? Well, I think the Peter Sellers character might have been based on Jenks.'

He had been standing still for some minutes – an unusually long time for him – but now, like a large carnivore in a small zoo cage, he began to pace.

'Are you going to expand on that?' she said.

'It's the roast pork business. By the way, I forgot to ask you what had happened to Raymond Naidoo.'

'Dodgy prawns I was told.'

'It's grotesque, isn't it?' The moment he gets food poisoning and can't come in, the whole bloody system falls apart. No one tells the agency nurse anything.'

'She's supposed to read the notes. She should have known Mason wasn't on any medication.'

'Well, they don't sometimes. Or don't take them in properly. Anyway the health-care staff are supposed to make sure she knows and Jenks is in control of the health-care staff.'

'And you're in control of Jenks.'

He stopped pacing and said, 'That's how it works. If the buck doesn't stop until it reaches me then the kicks up the backside should go on down the line, starting with Jenks. Fair's fair.'

'You sound like my father.'

'You've said that before and my admiration for him keeps growing.' He sat on the corner of his desk. 'But there is a silver lining. Jenks won't be calling any union meeting. Not if he doesn't want his own dereliction discussed.'

Normally, when Tom became tigrish, she had a clear feeling of wanting to avoid him until he returned to his usual character – the somehow cynical and slightly self-mocking person she had come to know – but she was pleased to find that what had happened – or nearly happened – in Wales had not changed him. She waited for him to continue but instead he said, 'Enough of that. Down with Jeffrey Jenks.' He paused. 'You wouldn't be making coffee would you?'

'Would you like a cup?'

'I thought you'd never ask.'

The Admiral stopped his car outside Lily's house. He stretched his arms on the steering wheel. 'Not much luck today, but we'll get there.'

'You really think so?' Lily said.

'Oh, yes, she must be there somewhere. We're doing it scientifically. We'll find her.'

When he spoke about Sandra she seemed to be a real person. When Mitchell had spoken about her, she hadn't.

The car was unfamiliar to Lily. It was large and the seats were leather and she felt its aura of richness. It was a nice feeling. She waited for Peter to get out but he didn't move. She'd assumed that he'd come in with her.

'Would you like a cup of tea?' she said, to break the ice.

'I don't think so thanks, Lily. I must be getting home. Lots of paperwork, I'm afraid.'

'Could I help? I used to be a secretary in a law office, you know.'

'I can manage. But thank you all the same.'

'Peter, would you ... I mean ... I wondered if you'd come round for dinner one evening.'

'I'd like to. Very much.'

'What night would suit you?'

'Can I look at my diary when I get home, and ring you?'

'Of course.'

'Of course' was a favourite phrase of his and she had found herself repeating it.

He touched her hand. 'Right then. I'll be in touch. And I'll let you know if anything happens in the search, of course.'

There it was again.

'And if that water-divining person comes along, I'd call the police if I were you,' he said.

'I thought I'd call you.'

He smiled. 'Yes. Do that. And just close the door in his face.'

She got out of the car. He raised a hand and drove off. He's tired, she thought, and goodness, so am I.

She took off her rubber boots and heavy socks and put the kettle on. She felt stiff and sore from walking. And sad. Sad because like the other working parties they had found nothing. So far the only thing that had been found of Sandra's was the handkerchief Mitchell *said* he'd found – and as Peter had said, it could have belonged to anyone.

She sat at the table sipping her tea. She had never met anyone like Peter before. 'Met' wasn't really the right word. She had certainly met admirals formally when Barry was alive: Mrs Benson, I'd like you to meet Admiral Sir Soandso-Soandso. That's all.

She had thought about the previous evening several times during the day, going over the events like rereading a lover's letters. It had been strange, because last night she had started thinking about sex again. She had become accustomed to a life of celibacy long ago and had stopped thinking about the sexual act except in a sentimental and nostalgic way. There had been a period after she had recovered from Barry's death when she had wondered if she would ever feel a man inside her again. Barry had been a bang-bang-turn-over-and-go-to-sleep man, and she had thought that was the normal way until she had heard other women talk.

A year after his death she had had a brief affair with a man who owned the garage in the neighbouring village. She hadn't enjoyed it much because he was married and had kids. He used to come to her house when Sandra was asleep – she'd have been six or seven then – and they'd done it on the couch in the living-room. She'd never allowed him into her bed.

And then . . . nothing. Years and years of nothing. Until last night.

She washed up her tea mug and then paused. It was time to go up to talk to Sandra. But just at the moment she didn't want to. She switched on the TV instead.

When Anne and Tom entered Roger Stimson's office he stubbed out his cigarette and waved his arms to clear the smoke.

'What have you got for me?' he said.

'About what?' Tom said.

'About the TV thing.' His manner was unusually tense and Anne thought he might have already heard about the roast pork fiasco.

'I'm trying to get hold of the girl, Sophie Lennox,' Tom said. 'Holroyd's putting out feelers. So far he hasn't come up with anything. Anne has been to Stepton to see if anyone has been approached by a TV company.'

He turned to Anne. 'And?'

'I haven't found out anything yet. Mason's mother and brother aren't exactly co-operative.'

'So that's all we've got. Well, we're going to need a bloody-sight more.' He held up a fax. 'This came half an hour ago. Taylor's dead.'

'You don't mean Harold Taylor?' Anne said.

'I do mean Harold Taylor. I mean the person who confessed to the crime Jameson was convicted of and who – do I have to go on?'

186

Anne said, 'How did he die?'

'I thought we might get to that. He was bloody murdered, that's how.'

'Oh Christ!' Tom said.

'I thought he was a rule forty-three,' Anne said.

'He was,' Stimson said. 'I phoned Barclay at The Hawes. He said Taylor was well separated from the others except – there's always a bloody exception isn't there? – except for half an hour yesterday. There was some maintenance work being done on the block. Don't ask me what happened because Barclay was waffling. I don't think he knows himself exactly what happened. Anyway, Taylor was stabbed with a sharpened screwdriver.'

The three of them were silent for a moment and then Stimson rubbed at his deep five-o'clock shadow and said, 'Well?'

'You're thinking of Mason Chitty?' Anne said.

'Precisely. I'm thinking that this will be all over the press, and for a man who has tried to kill himself once what will *he* be thinking? Won't he be frightened stiff of the same thing happening to him?'

'But Sandra Benson wasn't a juvenile,' Tom said.

Stimson said, 'Could be he's unbalanced enough not to know the difference. Look at the paracetamol. But how unbalanced? What I'm really saying is what sort of bloke is he? We don't know, do we? All we know is that he's charged with murder and he tried to top himself. And we can be bloody sure that if he succeeds next time we'll be the subject of a TV series all by ourselves, plus a departmental investigation, plus . . . well, you name it. So I ask myself, what are you going to do about him?'

'Us?' Tom's tone had become hard.

'He's in your hospital and with his track record I would have thought he'd have another go.'

Anne picked up Tom's mood. 'We've got him in almost total safety.'

'Almost?'

'Nothing's a hundred per cent.'

Tom said, 'If you're telling us to get our act together, let me say this: two of our main functions are to assess dangerousness and suicide risk. But doctors know little about either.'

'You mean your guess is as good as ours? Is that what you're saying, Tom? Aren't you forgetting the famous doctor – patient relationship?'

'And aren't you forgetting that Her Majesty's Chief Inspector of Prisons recently said that the new suicide prevention strategy isn't a medical problem, it's everybody's problem. Remember?'

They were all silent again; this time the silence was full of repressed antagonism. Anne broke it. 'I'll go back to Stepton,' she said. 'I'll *make* someone talk to me.'

18

'This is where he killed her,' Elizabeth Drayton said.

The room looked so innocuous to Anne's eyes. It was just a spare bedroom, the kind of room you found in rather grand but not very rich country houses. The furniture was old mahogany and through a door she could see a bathroom which had an old-fashioned chain-pull lavatory and a free-standing bath on ball-and-claw feet.

'He strangled her. He was a very powerful man and he used all his strength on her. There were accounts that said her eyes had almost come out. I imagine it was her bedroom then and she'd probably had Strudwick in her own bed. One doesn't know whether Sir James had been away and come back and found them, or what had happened. We don't even know whether Strudwick was killed first or whether it was Eleanor. In face there's not much known about it at all. It wasn't a fashionable murder, you see, just a man's wife sleeping with the groom. If Sir James and Eleanor had been a beautiful young couple, things might have been different, but they were middle-aged and, one has to say it, rather dowdy. That's her above the door and he's the one just left of the window.'

Anne looked at the portraits painted more than two hundred years before. They showed a dull-looking couple who were the direct forebears of Elizabeth Drayton.

'You ask most people in the village if there's ever been a murder in Stepton before – before Sandra Benson's, I mean – and they would probably say no. It never became famous in the way that some did.'

'What happened to Sir James?'

'He went out to the Cape of Good Hope for five or six years while his son looked after this estate. When he came back it had all blown over. I think the sentiment in those days was that a wife who slept with a groom had only herself to blame if she was throttled. Come down and have a drink.'

They went down to the room which Elizabeth called the little sitting-room and which had a large log smoking in the fireplace.

Anne said, 'I had tea just before I left the prison so I don't really want anything, thank you.'

Elizabeth helped herself to a whisky. It was not quite six o'clock on a windy May evening.

'You said on the phone you wanted to talk about Mason, but there really isn't very much I can tell you.'

Anne smiled. 'This village is becoming an English cliché.'

'How's that?'

190

'People not talking to what I suppose they'd call foreigners.'

Elizabeth had been standing at the fireplace. She was wearing a long, dark dress and her white hair was almost like a beautiful wig. Anne realised that its whiteness gave a feeling of age, yet if you looked more closely at her she was very well preserved. Now the dress flared as she swung round. She looked at Anne in silence for a moment.

'You might have been right thirty years ago. Perhaps even twenty. But not now, except I suppose for the old inhabitants. For the rest, the village is commuters and they don't know anything about the place.'

'They don't know about the Chitty family?'

'They don't know anything about anything except catching trains and paying the mortgage. Why should they? They all come from the tarmac jungle – that's the phrase, isn't it?'

'Something like that. But you know the Chittys. And you sold them some of your land, didn't you?'

'How do you know – oh, of course. I keep on forgetting you have Mason in your hospital.'

'I don't get much from him, but people do talk.'

'You're right, I did sell land to them. My God, I wonder what Dommie would have said.'

'Dommie?'

'Dominic, my late husband. He couldn't stand them. Couldn't stand most people if one was to be entirely honest.' She gave herself another whisky

191

and put very little water in it. 'You sure?'

'Yes, thanks. I'm sure.'

'I never argue with doctors. No, Dommie would have hated it, but the recession made it inevitable. It's the first time we've sold any land, I think. We always bought. But now people like me are the genteel poor. And he would have hated particularly selling it to the Chittys. Not quite his sort of people. I suppose I was once like that. Then after Rollo was killed in the Gulf War I thought: Oh, Christ, what's it all about?'

'What I was wondering was—'

'I mean, what the hell, I'm not a young deb any longer! And the country's changed out of all recognition. I'm all right, Jack, and everyone for himself: that's the style isn't it? And where's the shame? No such word any longer. Politicians caught in bed with tarts and they lie about it. Stock-exchange ramps: and when they're caught they lie about it. So to hell with it, I thought, and if people want to live like that then what's the matter with selling land to the Chittys? The problem was what they did with it.'

'Which was?'

'Built a bloody rubbish tip. People said they would but I thought they'd never get permission. But they did. Bribery, of course. Local government's even more corrupt than central and Samuel Chitty knows that. Mason wouldn't have done it and his father never, but Samuel would and probably did.

And now the old quarry that was part of the sale is filling up with Kingstown rubbish and the village hates them for doing it and me, probably, for selling them the land.'

'You said Mason wouldn't?'

'Well, it's not the sort of thing he would do.'

'They seem very different from one another,' Anne said. 'I meant their accents and their manners and their general behaviour.'

'Schooling. Mason was sent to a good boarding school near Brighton but Samuel went to the local comprehensive in Kingstown.'

'Any idea why?'

'They said Mason had been left some money by an aunt when he was a child. I know Harry, his father, was pleased as punch to see him get on.'

'Did you know the father?'

'Oh yes. He was a . . . I'm not sure quite how to describe him. I suppose some people would have called him a Jack-the-lad, but there was more to him than that. He seemed to enjoy life and that helps. He had a lorry in the old days; a lorry and a bit of land. Built everything up from there. Hired out the lorry and himself when he could and when he couldn't, worked the land. Loved horses, which was nice.'

'You make him seem very different from his wife. I've met her and Samuel a couple of times – once in court and once in their house – and they don't sound a bit like him. Nor like Mason.'

Elizabeth glanced at the whisky bottle, then seemed to decide against another drink. 'That was the mistake Harry made, marrying Florence. But you can understand it. She was much younger than he was and rather pretty. I remember her then. But what a background! If she hadn't been quite so . . . well, so Florence Chitty, one might have felt sorry for her. Her father was a wartime traitor. His ship was sunk by a U-boat early in the war. He was carted off to one of the Nazi prisoner-of-war camps and there he was turned from being a merchant seaman into a kind of internal spy. He spied on the other men, reported escape attempts, that sort of thing. At the end of the war he was shot by the men he'd betrayed. At that time the family was living in East Anglia but when the news of what happened reached there, Florence's mother took her daughter and came to settle here. I think Florence was badly scarred by all this so what she wanted was ultra respectability. Harry had just become a freemason – that's where Mason got his name – and that sounded very respectable to Florence. Samuel was born, and a year or so later, Mason. Harry doted on Mason, but when he died everything changed. Florence was much closer to Samuel and both of them were pretty bloody to Mason. It was just as well he was a teenager then or he might have been badly damaged.'

'And now it's Mason who's in trouble. That's ironic.'

Elizabeth shook her head. 'That's if he did it. They don't have a body.'

'The DNA found on him matches Sandra's.'

'So they keep saying, but I can't see it myself.'

'How's that?'

'Well, it's all mumbo jumbo really, isn't it? They talk in court about fingerprinting but it isn't that at all and—'

'That was explained. They had an expert witness and the judge explained it too.'

'Well, I must have missed it. I haven't been there every minute. Now the court tells us that it doesn't matter if there's no body because there's some blood on Mason and it's Sandra's!'

Anne wondered if her refusal to understand was the whisky or bloody-mindedness or ignorance or all three. Anne said, 'I had to be convinced too. But when I looked into it it made sense. The forensic scientist I spoke to said DNA was his most important weapon in the fight against crime since dusting for fingerprints. It's the blueprint for life; it tells us who we are and how we behave and how we look and everyone has a different blueprint which is identified when they analyse the blood. And they knew the blood was Sandra's because they compared it with some of her blood on file at the hospital and it was the same.'

Elizabeth shrugged and Anne said, 'Just one more thing then I must go. Did you know Sandra?'

'We *all* knew her. She grew up in the village.'

195

'I talked to her mother and she said she was a wonderfully sweet girl. Was that your feeling?'

'You've come to the wrong person. You really should talk to Betty Sugden. She was Sandra's great friend.'

'Where would I find her?'

'She lives with her grandmother near the shop, but I'm told she spends a lot of time with a horse coper called Mitchell.'

'In Stepton?'

'He's got a place on the Kingstown side of the village, a couple of miles out.'

Anne drove back through the village to the Kingstown road. As she passed the car-park she saw her father's large old Rover and assumed that he and Watch would be having a drink in the Mayfly. For a second she thought of joining them but she had to pick up Hilly so she drove on.

. . . well, was it yours, my love? I couldn't tell. I've got them like that and so have you. I checked in your drawer and you had five or six. It isn't as though it had initials on it. Just a white lady's handkerchief. And he said he could find things. I told you about the lock. Peter said he could have put it in the ground. But you don't carry things like that around, do you?'

I've been thinking about this a lot. What if he's right and it is yours? I should do something.

Did I tell you what Peter said? The trouble is, so

many things are happening to me nowadays that I forget what I've told you and what I haven't.

Did I tell you Peter came and had a drink? And we had a long chat about Mitchell and about you and about . . . oh, a lot of things . . . Yes, a lot of things.

Do you think I should go back to work? If I did I wouldn't be able to join the working party on weekdays. Peter's retired but it isn't often the others can come on a weekday. Of course, it'll be easier in summer when the days are longer.

Did I say 'of course'? Peter says it all the time. You used to say it. That . . . and Ooooh Mum!

Sandra . . . Sandra . . . I'd give anything to hear that again! Anything. My life.

She waits for the tears but they don't come.

I must go now, my darling, before it gets too dark. Just to look. There may be something . . .

It was past six o'clock when she left the house and walked up the gallops. Her eyes were on the ground long before she reached the area where the tapes blew in the wind. What was she looking for? A handkerchief? A ring? A bracelet?

She turned down onto the flat area between the Downs and the river, the area Treagust had described as the Burial Ground. Peter had jumped on him for that.

'Use what brains you have, man!' he'd said. The result was that Treagust had got huffy and hadn't come the next time the working party went out. Nor had Mitchell. Nor had Sandra's chum, Betty – but then she hadn't come at all. So it had only been Lily and Peter and, of course – there was that phrase again – Kenny.

The wind had come up and was blowing in off the Channel. There was dampness in the air. It was gloomy and she was sorry she'd come out, but she had told Sandra she was going to make a search and now she had to. She turned away from the river and moved into the woods, the big beech trees towered above her.

This is where things would lie unfound she thought, here under the deep, damp mould of leaves and grass. It hardly made any sound as she walked on it. But where? She kicked some of the leaf mould. Anywhere . . . that was the point. Anything could be anywhere. And so could her darling. She could be here under the leaf mould, stiff and dead.

'Oh God!' The words came bursting from her throat.

She was looking at a man. He was standing by a tree trunk only a few feet away from her yet she could hardly make him out. He seemed black all over.

'Oh God!'

He put out a hand as though to touch her or ward her off.

She screamed.

He turned and began to lumber away. Another man came towards her from a different direction. He was white and she thought she had seen him before. Both of them, in fact.

The white man said, 'It's all right, Mrs Benson. No one's going to hurt you.'

'Cheers,' Henry Vernon said, raising his glass. Watch did not respond and Mrs Benson was, Henry thought, lukewarm.

They were in the snug of the Mayfly and Henry took a large mouthful of his whisky and soda, let it gargle around the back of his tongue, then swallowed it with satisfaction. There were some occasions when drinks tasted better than others and this was one of them.

'You frightened the life out of Watch,' he said to Lily. 'It was the scream that did it.'

Watch was looking glassy-eyed at the drink he held in his hands. It was a brandy and water and now he raised it to his lips and drained it. He made a low hissing noise which upset Lily and she said, 'Well, he frightened the life out of me. And so did you.'

'I've explained all that,' Henry said. 'And I've explained who I am and—'

'You said you're a judge.'

'Was . . . was a judge. I've retired now. Anyway, you know all about us and who my daughter is – indeed, you've met her. And you know who Watch is, too. You know he's not some wild savage who is going to knock you down and—'

'Please . . .' Lily said.

'Well, I wanted to get the parameters set because there's something I need to say to you.'

'I'm not sure I want to hear it.'

'It's about Sandra.'

She pushed her drink away. 'I won't listen . . . I don't talk about her to anyone.'

'Oh, yes, you do,' Henry said. 'We've been doing some talking ourselves. Talking and listening.'

Lily began to rise. 'I don't have to . . .'

'Please, Mrs Benson, all we want to do is to help you.'

'How much?'

'What?'

'How much do you want for your help? Fifty pounds? A hundred?'

Watch moved uncomfortably. 'We do not eh-want money,' he said.

'What's it all about then?' Lily was surprised at the tone of her own voice.

'I'll tell you what it's all about,' Henry said, and sketched in briefly what had so far occurred and Watch's interest in helping to find her daughter.

Lily's face changed from irritation to apprehension, to disbelief, then to an uneasy concentration.

'He uses bones?' she said at last.

'Animal bones,' Henry said, not wishing to send her fleeing off home. 'It's well known in Africa. Like reading cards or tea-leaves here. The point is, would you accept an offer of help in what is – as I understand it – a search that's going nowhere?'

'That's not true. Admiral Pattinson says it's early days yet and he should know. He's an admiral!'

Henry was unimpressed. 'I'm sure he knows a great deal about the sea but why should he know anything about finding a dead body on land?'

'He . . . he just does. We have working parties. And we have tapes.'

'But haven't the police been over the ground with their sophisticated equipment?'

'They can't search everywhere.'

'Well, now we have a new factor in the equation – Watch.'

Watch looked down at his empty glass.

'When he touched you he says he felt an aura.'

'Oh, God!'

'It was quite a strong feeling.'

'Listen, I don't—'

'Mrs Benson, I understand you could have doubts about us, and if you do, you can check on us with Mrs Drayton.'

Lily was surprised. 'Mrs Dray—Elizabeth? What's she got to do with it?'

Henry gave her another brief background sketch but confined Watch's mishap to a branch blown by the wind.

201

In spite of herself Lily was interested.

'Watch needs something of your daughter's,' Henry said. 'Something he can touch, feel, hold.'

'What sort of something?'

'Clothing,' Watch said.

'Nothing intimate.' Henry was quick to reassure her.

'A handkerchief?'

'That would be fine wouldn't it, Watch?'

'Yes, yes, very good.'

'I have one here.'

From her handbag Lily took out a white handkerchief and passed it to Watch. It was the one Mitchell said he'd found.

19

'There's a message!' Hilly's voice came down the stairs. 'Can I take it?'

Anne, putting things away in the kitchen, called back, 'No, I'm coming up.'

'You *never* let me!'

'Hop it.'

Anne switched on the machine. It was Tom. 'I have something for you. Remember the nurse I told you about in Kingstown General whose mother was a district nurse years ago in Stepton? Sorry about that sentence, I've had two glasses of wine. Anyway, she's going to ring you. The mother that is, not the daughter. The daughter says it's no use you ringing her mother because she's out in the garden most of the time. And there's something else. Holroyd's found out Sophie Lennox is working out of Southampton. He doesn't have a number for her yet but he's optimistic. Why don't you give me a ring and tell me what you've been up to? I'm in all evening. And since I am your immediate superior you can take that as an order. 'Bye.'

She went downstairs. His voice was still in her ears. It had been full of the amused self-mockery she liked. It reminded her of when she was a houseman (housewoman?) at St Thomas's Hospital in London. There had been the usual group of very earnest young doctors but there had also been the unearnest ones who took their jobs seriously but had the ability to laugh at themselves.

Hilly was sitting at the kitchen table, drawing.

'What do you want for supper?' Anne said.

'Please can I not have haddock?'

'Of course you needn't. How about a cheese omelette?'

Hilly was eating her omelette when Henry and Watch returned. Henry said, 'What's that?'

'Cheese omelette,' Hilly said.

'Looks splendid.'

Watch tottered down to his room.

'I'll make you one if you like,' Anne said. 'Will Watch have one too?'

'I shouldn't think so. He's had the most enormous meal you ever saw. Something called lascania. Mince and horrid white dough.'

'No such thing. Probably lasagne. And it's very nice.'

'Doesn't sound like British pub food to me. You used to be able to get decent things like toad in the hole and Scotch eggs and bangers and mash, now you get things like this lascania, and Mexican slops and tandoori this and tandoori that. Whatever happened to British cooking?'

'Sit down and have a British *omelette au fromage*. I saw your car in Stepton. I was at Mrs Drayton's.'

'You should have stopped for some delicious lascania.'

'Had to pick up Hilly.' She beat the eggs. 'How do you like it, wet or dry?'

'Medium dry.'

They ate together.

'We weren't only there for the ghastly lascania,' Henry said, and then told her how they had met Lily. 'You said you knew her.'

'I hardly *know* her. I told you, she wanted to see me about getting Mason to tell her where he'd buried Sandra – that's if he *had* killed her.'

'Now she's got a firm offer of help.'

'You're making fun of Watch. You don't believe him for a second. I think it's cruel.'

Henry held up his hand for silence. 'Listen . . .'

There came the faintest click of the bones being thrown against the wall of his bedroom.

Henry went on, 'I'm not making fun of him and I'm just as worried about him as you are. More so because I've known him and liked him for so long. I've had to come to terms with something I should have realised when he first arrived – Kingstown isn't Maseru.'

'I told you that.'

'That's not the same as realising it oneself. And there's something else. A great many strange things happen on a daily basis in Africa, things that don't happen here. I'm talking about their beliefs, their oral traditions, their tribal memories. Last night I couldn't sleep and I went back to some of my books on Lesotho. Its history really is remarkable. On the one side there has been cannibalism and ritual murder but on the other the great leader Moshesh who defeated a British army by flattery and diplomacy and talked his nation into becoming a colony ruled and protected by Queen Victoria. He said he and his people were "the lice in the Queen's blanket". And later it became an independent black country in the middle of a white racist one. It's fantastic, really.'

'What's that got to do with Watch?'

'He's a product of it all. For years and years I only judged him in his role as legal clerk. I never fitted him into his background. He had to fit into mine. Now the point is that if he feels he can help to find Sandra, why shouldn't he try? Mrs Benson desperately wants to find her body and mourn. If Watch can help her, then it helps them both.'

Anne said, 'How did Mrs Benson react?'

'Rather well, I thought. When Watch said he needed something of Sandra's she gave us her handkerchief.'

'I hope you didn't raise her expectations.'

'I told her the truth. But they're not getting anywhere with their own searches. The barman at the pub told me that what they call the working parties are getting smaller and fewer in number. All they've done is plaster the landscape with that red plastic tape. There's some old admiral in charge and it all sounds like he's organising the battle of Jutland.'

The phone rang. Anne thought for a moment it might be the ex-district nurse Tom had mentioned but it was Tom's ex-wife, Stephanie. 'I'll take it upstairs,' she said, and went up to her bedroom.

'I thought so often of ringing you,' Stephanie said. 'But I say to myself why will Anne want to hear from me?'

Anne kept silent. The French-accented voice was soft and friendly.

'Can you hear me?'

'Yes. What can I do for you?'

There was a dry gurgle of laughter. 'All doctors are the same. What can I do for you? It is what Tom used to say.'

'I'm afraid—'

'No, no, of course, you are busy. Doctors are always busy. Tom was busy. My father was a doctor, so I know what it means.'

'I'm putting my daughter to bed.'

'We never had a child. The time was never correct. You know something? Tom does not like children. He did not want one. I said, but darling what is marriage without children? So you are lucky to have a child. No one can take that away from you.'

'Is there something you want?' Anne pictured the small and slender woman with the Mediterranean colouring, the high-cheekboned face, the dark-brown eyes and the crimped black hair.

'We always want something, *n'est-ce pas*? And always something that is difficult. I want Tom. And I want him to make me pregnant. I want to be part of a family again. People like you may not understand such a thing.'

'Sorry?'

'Perhaps you do not think about it because you have it.'

'Have what?'

'What I want.'

'Look, Mrs Melville. I can't—'

'You can call me Stephanie.'

'I'd rather call you Mrs Melville and really, I think I must end this. There's nothing I can do for you and—'

'There is something.'

'What?'

'You can take your hands off Tom.' The original soft tone was only a memory.

'That's it!' Anne said.

'Don't hang up, you bitch! I am in Kingstown. If you hang up I shall come to your house. And do not think I will not come. I know where you live. Castle Street. Just on the bend.'

Anne had a sudden sickening feeling of having been watched.

'Tom and I we marry in church. It is for ever. You think you can take him? You can take nothing from me. Nothing.' Her syntax was beginning to slip.

Anne wanted desperately to put down the receiver but the thought of this woman coming to the house was so awful she could not contemplate it. She suddenly tried to visualise Stephanie as a female counterpart of the prisoner Monks, irrational, pressurised, angry. And as soon as she did, Stephanie was reshaped into a lonely and half-demented woman; neither strong nor dangerous. The diagnostic side of Anne's character listened as she might have listened to a prisoner whom she was assessing for treatment in a secure hospital. 'Go on,' she said.

'On? What is on, you bitch?'

'You were telling me about how much you needed Tom. Go on.'

'Hey . . . what is this? What are you doing?'

'I'm listening.'

'I know that tone of voice. I know what you are doing. You think I'm going to stand for this?'

'Stand for what, Mrs Melville?'

'Don't talk to me like that. I'm not . . .' she paused.

'Not what, Mrs Melville?'

'You think you're very clever but you're stupid. Stupid! You think Tom wants a stupid woman?'

'Do *you* think he wants a stupid woman, Mrs Melville?'

'I know what you did. You take him to his child's bed and you fuck him. You think his mother don't know?'

Anne felt something catch alight inside her but
she managed to hold the fire in check. 'Do I think
his mother knows what?'

'I spoke to her on the phone. She told me you
were there. But I knew it already. I phoned Tom in
his room last night and he took the phone away.
You think I don't know why? In his own room he
has had since a child! You're a terrible person, you
know that, and stupid.'

'Yes, you've said that, Mrs Melville.'

'Don't talk to me like I'm a . . . a . . . Wait . . . just
wait till I come to your house. Wait until I tell your
old father and your child.'

'Listen carefully to me. In my job I know many
senior police officers and when I put down the
phone I'm going to ring one and tell him what you've
just said to me. He won't do anything extreme but
if you were to come here, for instance, a car would
arrive in a minute or two and they would take you
away. Have you any idea what a woman's prison is
like? No? Not very nice, I'm told and—'

'Bitch!'

'Sticks and stones, Mrs Melville. Do you have a
similar phrase in French?'

There was a click as the other receiver was
replaced. Anne put hers down slowly. She
was feeling a mixture of an adrenalin rush and
disgust. For a moment she thought of phoning
Tom but he'd be hideously embarrassed and what
could he do? It was possible, anyway, that she might

have scared Stephanie into silence.

She went downstairs. Her father was where she had left him. He was sucking at his pipe and the room was filled with the smell of latakia and the sound of small drains.

'Who was that?'

'Some woman who knows my boss. She wants him ... What were we talking about? Oh yes, I remember. What were you doing at Mrs Drayton's?'

The phone rang again. 'Oh, God,' Henry said. 'Can't they ring in office hours?'

Anne picked up the phone, feeling the adrenalin rush once more. An elderly voice said, 'It's Mrs Timmins.'

'Who?'

'Are you the doctor who wants to know about the old times in Stepton? My daughter said I was to call.'

'Yes ... yes ... that's me. I wonder if I could come to see you?'

The bedroom is cold. The heating is turned off. She sees specks of dust on the glass top of Sandra's dressing-table and realises she has not cleaned it for more than two days.

She sits on the chair in the middle of the room and feels a chill in her legs. Today she does not know how to begin. Most times it is easy, she simply starts talking. In the beginning, of course, she talked and cried most of the day. This time she has started talking and has got into a muddle.

So she begins again . . . A black man . . . I've never sat down with one before. It was odd. But that was all. I remember your father saying they were just like everyone else. And it's true. But you don't meet them in Stepton.

The other man was a judge.

People might say I'm foolish, but I sort of trusted them. I was going to phone Peter but then I thought, no. He said not to let Mitchell try. I've regretted that. I think I would've let him if I'd had the money. You see, my love, the Judge said the working parties aren't getting very far, and he's right. There were four to start with, only two now and Mike Treagust is cross and Betty never came at all. Mitchell didn't come the last time, either. I suppose because I haven't been in touch.

So I thought: why not?

You remember old Mrs Hickman? She used to tell fortunes. I took you there once and she said you'd grow up into a beautiful, kind person, which you did.

Ooooh Mum!

Anyway, that's how good a fortune teller can be. Old Mrs Hickman used to tell fortunes with cards and tea-leaves and sometimes she'd look in a person's hand and tell them how long they would live.

She never looked in yours, my love.

There it was. The ache. It ambushed her when

she least expected it. Go on. Talk!

Well, the Judge said that in this place in Africa they throw bones and they read the future in bones. And he said that the black man had touched me – I don't remember that but he said it was at the Mayfly when I spoke to his daughter the doctor – and when he touched me he felt an aura. That's what he told the Judge.

I've looked up 'aura' and I brought the dictionary here so I could read it to you . . . It says: 'a supposed subtle emanation, especially that essence which is claimed to emanate from all living things and to afford an atmosphere for occult phenomena.'

That's what it says in the dictionary and I thought, all right, if the black man is really a psychic – except I'm sure there's another name for them in this African place – then maybe . . . maybe . . . he can help . . .

And they know Elizabeth Drayton, so they must be all right.

213

20

'... his grandfather on his mother's side,' Anne said. 'Apparently he was some sort of spy for the prison camp authorities and he was shot by British prisoners at the end of the war.'

'And people in his village knew?' Tom asked.

'So Mrs Drayton said. That's why the family moved from East Anglia to Sussex. It's not the best background.'

'It shouldn't matter after all this time. Would you like another?' He held up his glass.

'No thanks.'

They were in the King's Arms in Kingstown. The dim interior was almost empty and through the windows Anne could see the tables outside where they had sat in the warm early spring days. Those days had gone now and it was a more typical English spring of wind and rain and racing clouds.

'I think I will,' he said. 'You sure?'

'I'm sure.'

He got up and went towards the bar, but came back and sat down without refreshing his glass.

'The phrase in the movies is: We can't go on like this,' he said.

For a second she didn't understand. 'Like what?'

'Like not talking about anything. Like pretending nothing happened. It did happen. Or would have happened if things had been allowed to take their course.'

'But it didn't.'

'What I'm saying is . . . look, both of us knew exactly what we were doing. It might not have happened in a real physical sense but it did emotionally.'

Pause.

'Or don't you think so?' he said.

'I'm not sure I want to analyse it.'

'Oh, come on. It's going to be in our minds all the time we work together, or go away to conferences.' He picked up his empty glass and stared down at the droplets in the bottom. 'In which case it'd be a totally false, even an artificial relationship.'

'I know. That's what I'm afraid of.'

'So we're to pretend it never happened?'

'No, I don't mean that.'

'What then?'

'I don't know. I'm no expert on this kind of thing. I just am very wary of it. Say we had an affair which broke up in acrimony. What then? How would we go on with our present lives? I like my job. I have Hilly at school here. I have my father living with us. And now his old clerk, Watch. In some ways it would be marvellous to forget all of them for a while and just indulge myself. But . . .' she stopped and raised her shoulders.

'But me no buts,' Tom said, and they both smiled stiffly. Then he said, 'Are you thinking of Paul?'

Her silence was assent and he went on, 'I have a feeling that whenever some sort of relationship peers over the horizon you start thinking of him.'

'Maybe.'

'You've got to let him go, Anne.'

'I know.'

In her mind's eye she saw Paul's body, crushed and broken. He had been the architect in charge of an extension to the hospital at which she was working. That was how they had met and fallen in love and she had conceived Hilly. Then a site crane had toppled in a gale and he had been underneath it. She had been in Casualty when they'd brought him in.

'It's understandable that you get caught up in memories, but that's what they are, nothing more.'

'Hilly's a fairly strong memory.'

'Hilly is Hilly.'

'She's also what's left of Paul.'

They were silent for some moments, neither knowing how to continue a conversation that was getting away from them.

'What is it you want, Tom?'

'Generally?' She nodded. 'Well, I suppose what most people want: wife . . . kids . . . happiness.'

'But you don't like children.'

'What?'

'Sorry, I thought . . .'

'No, please, I'd like to know what brought that on. You've seen me with Hilly and—'

Absolutely. No, no, I wasn't thinking . . .'

'Christ, you haven't been – Stephanie hasn't been on to you, has she? That's the sort of thing she'd say. Has she?'

'She phoned last night. Look, I'm very, very sorry. It – it slipped out.'

'It was in your mind. Planted there for just such an opportunity. And it explains quite a lot of this conversation. What did she phone about anyway?'

'You, mainly.'

'Oh, Lord. What have I done now?'

'It's what you haven't done. You haven't gone back to her. And she blames me.'

'I'm very flattered. I'm also rather concerned. Steffie can be a loose cannon. I wasn't going to tell you but I might as well now: she came to Mother's house a few hours after we'd left which is why I guessed it was she who'd planted that seed. Mother phoned and told me she'd gone into my bedroom looking for us. She seemed to know you'd been there – or else Mother told her – I'm not sure which. Anyway, it was unpleasant but it could have been worse because by that time Roberto had arrived and Mother had an ally.'

'When did she leave Kilvert?'

'She was there last night. I'm not even sure she's left now.'

'She said she was in Kingstown. And that she

was going to come round and . . . and I'm not quite
sure what.'

'So what did you do?'

'I went into my best psychiatric act and when
that didn't work I threatened to call the police if
she made any trouble. I wasn't going to tell you
because . . . well, because I didn't want to worry
you and I'm sure it was a one-off.'

'Our relationship was supposed to be over and
done with. Something that had happened in the
past. God, I'm sorry you had to put up with her.'

'You see, we both have problems about the past.'

'But in different ways.'

'What do you call this place?' Henry waved at the
landscape.

Lily thought: the Burial Ground. The phrase
Mike Treagust had used had remained in her mind
but she said, 'I don't know that it has a name, it's
just called Stepton Farm or Mrs Drayton's farm.'

They were in the area which Henry thought of
as 'the water meadows'. Except that they weren't
water meadows. The land could not be described
as meadows for it was rough and unlovely, nor was
there any water. But it was near the river.

Lily was looking at Watch. He had parted from
them some minutes before and was walking slowly
towards the stand of trees where he had been struck
in the face by a wind-tossed branch – that was how
the incident was now identified. He was leaning

ALAN SCHOLEFIELD

into the wind and she could see in his hand the white handkerchief.

'You've been in the search parties,' Henry said. 'What were you looking for . . . as clues, I mean?'

'Disturbed ground. Nettles.'

'Nettles?'

'Peter . . . the Admiral . . . said nettles are supposed to grow in disturbed ground.'

'I've never heard of that, but we didn't get nettles in Africa. Not as far as I can remember, anyway. We might as well look around while Watch is on the go. Why don't I try over there?' He gestured towards the edge of what had once been a ploughed field. 'She doesn't look after her place, does she?'

'It's the recession, and her son was killed in the Gulf War. That's when she started selling land to the Chittys.'

'Do you want to go in the other direction?' he said.

But she didn't. Suddenly she didn't want to be searching by herself. 'I'll come with you.'

As they reached the edge of the weed-covered field she said, 'This is called "set-aside" now. The owners are paid not to farm it.'

'My God, what an irony!'

Watch had gone into the wood.

Lily said, 'Can he really find things?'

'I have to say I don't know. I'm not even sure he knows. But it's worth letting him try, isn't it?'

There was something about Henry that appealed to Lily. He was four-square – she could hear Barry

220

using the phrase – and he seemed to contain in him the attributes of a trustworthy uncle.

'Yes, it's worth it,' she said.

They began to cross the broken field. Henry twirled a stick in his hand. Peter always carried a metal rod and he poked it into the ground. She believed Peter's way was the more practical but there was an ebullience about Henry's movements that she liked.

After a few minutes he pointed to a Land-Rover on the Downs. 'There's someone coming.'

It stopped near them and Mitchell got out.

He was bigger and taller than Lily remembered. He came towards her across the lumpy ground and said, 'You still looking?'

'Yes. I'm still looking.'

Henry was standing with his stick lying across the back of his neck, his hands on either end.

'This is Mr Vernon,' she said.

Mitchell nodded briefly, still watching Lily. 'You thought about what we talked over?'

She wasn't sure how to answer. She wished Peter was there to talk for her, he was good at that.

She said, 'I'm thinking.'

He glanced at Henry. 'You getting more help?'

'Mr Vernon is just a . . . a friend. He came out to keep me company.'

Mitchell seemed to accept the lie. He said, 'You want to think hard. I can find her. She's here somewhere.'

221

He flung out an arm to embrace the area and at that moment Watch reappeared from the wood.

'Who the hell's that black bugger?' Mitchell said.

'He's with us,' Henry said.

Mitchell ignored him and walked towards Watch. 'Who are you?' he shouted.

Watch stopped.

'I told you he was with us,' Henry said in a voice that had chilled the hearts of guilty parties over the years.

Mitchell seemed not to hear him. He said suddenly, 'Where the hell did you get that, you black sod?'

Watch looked down at the white handkerchief in his hand, at which Mitchell was pointing.

'Mind your mouth,' Henry said.

Again Mitchell ignored him. He turned to Lily. 'Is that the hankie I found?'

'Yes, it is.'

'Did you give it to him?'

'He's a psychic. He's trying to—'

Mitchell advanced until he was only a few feet away from her. 'Don't talk soft! A psychic? A black bugger like him? How much you paying him?'

'Not a penny!' Lily was angry now.

She was almost Mitchell's height. Her face was flushed and her heavy dark hair was blown back in the wind. Henry saw with surprise that she looked handsome and somewhat formidable.

Mitchell said, 'Well, *you* find her then. You and

this black sod. You find her! But don't come back to me, mind. Don't come to me!' He climbed into the Land-Rover and drove across the field towards the Downs, zigzagging past the dane-holes at fifty miles an hour.

'I'm sorry,' Lily said to Watch. 'I'm really sorry.'

'It's not the first time, Mrs Benson,' Henry said. 'And it won't be the last. Watch knows that. So do I.' He twirled his stick as though to clear the air and then said to Watch, 'Any luck?'

Watch folded the handkerchief and gave it back to Lily. 'It tell me nothing,' he said.

21

Her name was Olive, that much Anne remembered. But she couldn't have put a face to the name. She had just seen her as a figure coming out of the shop when Anne had bumped into Kenny. It was a small shop, part post office. When she had called in before there had been a queue of women waiting to be served; now it was empty. Olive was behind the counter writing out accounts. She was a thin woman with a long face and blue-rinsed grey hair. She wore a flowery overall and glasses on a cord. She looked up as Anne entered. Her eyes opened with surprised recognition, then went blank.

'Can I help you?' she said.

Anne introduced herself and reminded her of their previous meeting.

'Yes, I remember.'

'I wonder if I could ask you a couple of questions?'

'Oh?'

'I'm a medical officer at the prison. I'm looking after Mason Chitty.'

'Yes.'

'I've come here to try and find out a bit about Mason's background.'

She waited for an acknowledgement but Olive said nothing.

'You know him, of course.'

'They have an account at this shop. I know all the Chittys.'

'Could you tell me something about Mason's life. Perhaps his earlier years?' She found herself floundering under the shopkeeper's hard gaze.

'I've only been here nine years.'

'So you wouldn't have known him as a child, I realise that. But later on—'

'What kind of things do you want to know?'

'Well, what sort of person was he?'

'A very nice sort of person.'

'Did he get on with his brother Samuel?'

'You'd have to ask him that. Or his mother.'

Anne knew that Olive was retreating into the classic secretiveness of the English villager when questioned by an outsider. She would probably lie about the time of day if she was asked, yet Kenny's mother had said she knew everything that went on.

Anne decided to switch subjects. 'I'm looking for Betty Sugden. Could you tell me where she lives?'

An expression of relief passed over Olive's long face. 'Kenny will show you, won't you, Kenny?'

Startled, Anne turned. Kenny was standing just behind her. He had opened the door, crossed the shop and she had heard nothing.

'Hello, Kenny,' she said. 'How are you?'

Kenny's young-old face with its beige-tinted skin stared at her in what seemed incomprehension. He was more than ten years older than she was, yet she found herself treating him as though he was a child.

Olive said, 'Kenny, show the doctor to old Mrs Sugden's house.'

'Brrriiimm-brriiimm . . .' said Kenny.

'Just one thing more,' Anne said. 'Have you seen any TV people around here, making a film or asking questions?'

Olive ignored her and said, 'Kenny, tell your mum her pension book has come in.'

'Brrooom-brooom.' Kenny turned to the door.

'You'd better hurry, doctor, if you want Kenny to show you Mrs Sugden's house. He rides very fast.'

Anne followed Kenny on foot. He led her past the Mayfly and away from the river. He turned up a small lane, stopped in front of a tiny thatched cottage and pointed.

'Thank you, Kenny.'

'Brrriiiimmmmm—'

She was alone. The village seemed far away even though she was not far from its centre. Here, trees cut off sight and almost all sound of it.

The cottage was the kind people dream of owning – except that it was a semi-ruin. She estimated it was hundreds of years old, built of a mixture of flint and brick, with a thatched roof. But the thatch had been neglected. Large swathes had been blown down and lay on the ground at one side; that still remaining on the roof was corrugated and of differing shades. There was no garden and the brick path to the door was slippery with moss.

For a moment she was tempted to turn away, then she remembered Mason and her conversations with the governor and Tom.

She went to the door and knocked. An ancient, strident voice called, 'Is that you, Betty?'

She knocked again and called, 'No, it's not Betty.'

The door was opened by a small, shrivelled woman in her seventies.

'Yes?'

'I'm looking for Betty Sugden. I was told she lives here.'

'That's a joke,' the old woman said.

'You're Mrs Sugden?'

'I'm her grannie, that's what I am. Though you wouldn't know it from the way she behaves.'

A smell of ancient cooking was coming through the door.

'Can you tell me where she is?'

'Some bar somewhere. Some dance-hall.'

Anne hadn't heard anyone use the word dance-hall, though she had seen it in books.

'A disco?' she said. 'During the day?'

The old lady glared at her. 'What d'you want her for?'

'Just to talk to her.'

'What about?'

Anne hesitated.

Mrs Sugden said, 'When you find her, you tell her I wants to talk to her, too. She's taken my burial fund money.'

'Your what?'

'She was here yesterday. When she left, the money was gone. You tell her I wants it. It isn't fair. I mean, I looked after her when she was young but now I'm old she don't look after me. All she wants is money. And things to wear. To go to them dance-halls in. Silk. My God, and her father a tractor driver and her mother a cleaner. Silk!'

'Thanks, Mrs Sugden. Sorry to have bothered you.' Anne began to back down the path.

'You tell her I want my money!' Mrs Sugden shouted after her.

She found herself in the lane and walked quickly to the village. She remembered Elizabeth Drayton telling her that Betty was also living with a horse dealer called Mitchell and when she saw a postman emptying one of the big red letterboxes she asked for directions to his place. As she drove up the road she could see the Chittys' house on her left. Their land was sandwiched between Mitchell's and Mrs Drayton's. In the distance, near the river, she could just make out a small figure. It seemed to be running in a large circle. She pulled up for a moment to watch and realised that it was Kenny riding his invisible motorbike.

She drove on and soon Mitchell's place came into view.

It was in a hollow of the Downs. Anne, for most of the short drive, had been able to see the Drayton and the Chitty farms on her left. Now, abruptly, she turned a right-hand bend and entered a small valley.

A series of flint barns lay a little off the road and she turned towards them. As she drew near she saw that the house itself was a converted barn. A huge mound of manure and straw from which came a heavy, horsy smell, was piled alongside the barns which had been turned into stables.

Many seemed unoccupied, their doors standing open, but she could see horses in others, one in particular bobbing its head in an endlessly repetitive movement.

There were two elderly tractors nearby, a lorry of the same vintage, and three or four large pieces of broken farm machinery. As she pulled up she saw a silver Mercedes station wagon. It was parked in one of the barns and by the look of it could not be more than a couple of years old.

She went to the house and before she could raise her hand to knock, the door was opened and a young woman said, 'You want something?'

'Betty?'

She was about twenty, much the same age as Sandra would have been, dark, petite and very pretty in a doll-like way. Her short hair was tinted and so stiff with spray that it was almost moulded around a face which was heavily made up. She wore leopard-skin-printed leggings under a loose, thigh-length silk shirt which looked expensive.

'Is it about a horse? Mr Mitchell isn't home.'

'If you're Betty Sugden, I've come to see you.'

Betty's eyes were immediately hostile and Anne recalled the missing burial fund money. 'It won't take long,' she said. 'You have nothing to worry about.' She told Betty who she was.

'You better come in then. But there's precious little I can tell you about Mason.'

She led Anne into the sitting-room. The stereo was on and there was a blast of heavy rock music from two big, uncovered speakers which were fixed to the wall on either side of the fireplace. The furniture looked as though it had been bought from a mail-order brochure a long time ago. Copies of *Hello!* Magazine lay on a stained table.

'You knew Mason, of course,' Anne said.

'Why of course?'

'Sorry. That didn't have a hidden meaning. It's just that you're from the same village.'

Betty lit a cigarette with an expensive Dunhill lighter. She inhaled and blew out the smoke in a thin line.

'We don't all live in each other's pockets.'

'I'm sure you don't. May I sit down?'

She didn't wait for Betty to agree but seated herself in one of the 'cottage-style', rug-covered chairs that stood in front of the fireplace. From it she could see through to the kitchen. An old, chipped sink was filled with unwashed dishes.

'I'm trying to help Mason,' she said. 'Anything you can tell me might be useful.'

Betty sat on the sofa and pulled up her legs. Her feet were bare and there was a tattoo on her left ankle. Her doll-like face had fallen into a truculent expression. Anne had not enjoyed her discussion with either Olive or Mrs Drayton. In a way they had seemed to think that since she was treating Mason she shared his guilt – if indeed there was guilt. She decided she was not going to endure another such conversation.

'You were Sandra's friend, weren't you?'

'Yeah.' The tone was suspicious.

'And I've been told you grew up together and went to school together and were very close.'

'What're you getting at?'

'Is that true?'

'Yeah, I suppose so.'

'So you must have been devastated when she was killed.'

'Of course I was. Why are you asking me questions like this?'

'Because I just want to know why you didn't tell all you knew about Mason.'

'Here! Who the hell d'you think you are? You come in, you sit down without being asked and now you call me a liar. I didn't lie!'

'You would have known they were having an affair. At least you could have said that much.'

'Nobody asked me!'

'Well, I'm asking you and not only about that. Remember you're not talking to a policeman or a lawyer. There's nothing I can do to harm you. All I'm trying to do is help Mason, someone you know, someone who comes from the village, and someone who may be going to prison for a long time for something he might not have done.'

'What's it to you?'

'I don't like people being punished for the wrong reasons. Especially when it might involve wrongful imprisonment.'

'You said it again. How do you know? You don't know everything!'

Anne had a memory of Lily Benson saying much the same thing.

'Do *you*?' Anne said.

'What sort of question is that? You're a stranger. You come here where Sandra was killed and you think you know every bloody thing. Mrs Benson thinks Mason did it. So does half the village. So where do you get off talking to me like that?'

'But that's the point. What you're saying is that because some people think he's guilty then he's guilty and to hell with evidence or a court case. And it seems a lot easier in a village where the Chittys aren't exactly popular. What you've got to work out is whether someone should go to prison for life just because you and a few other people *think* he's guilty . . . Can't you switch that damn thing off!'

'Sorry.' She switched off the heavy rock. Her whole expression, even her demeanour, had changed. The truculence and antagonism had been replaced by apprehension and doubt.

'That's better. Now I can hear you,' Anne said.

'Do you think he will go to jail? You know, for life?'

'If he's found guilty, yes.'

'Oh Christ!'

Anne waited for her to say something more but she lit another cigarette instead.

'Would it worry you if he went down for life?'

'Not if he killed Sandra.'

'We may never know whether he did or didn't because people like you don't speak up.'

'They never asked me if I knew whether Mason and Sandra were having an affair.'

'But you did know. You could have told someone. The police, for instance.'

'I wasn't even here.'

'Where were you?'

'Away.'

She was twisting the lighter and her body was stiff with tension. 'Anyway Sandra didn't want nobody to know.'

'Was she ashamed?'

'Well, he was older, wasn't he, and—'

'And?'

'Because it's a village and there's talk.'

Anne leaned back in the rocker and said, 'Tell me about Sandra.'

Betty looked at her sharply. 'What do you want to know?'

'What was she like. Her mother told me one version. Then I asked Mrs Drayton. She was the one who said I should ask you.'

'The bitch! She just wants to get me into trouble.'

'Why?'

'Because of Rollo.'

'Who is Rollo?'

'You never heard of our war hero?'

'You mean Mrs Drayton's son?'

'Yeah. She always thought he was too good for the likes of us.'

The story came out in snatches, a story not uncommon, Anne thought, in English villages where children of differing classes played together when tiny, only to be separated when they grew older. Rollo and Betty had been close friends when they were at the village school together. Then Rollo had gone off to boarding school and Betty had remained in the state system. There was an echo here of Mason and Samuel.

Betty flicked the lighter several times and looked at the flame, then she said, 'It didn't bloody work did it? Her trying to keep him away from us. When he left school and his father died he didn't have to

235

take that shit any more. He joined the Air Force and came back at weekends.'

'And?'

'We had a good time. Rollo and me and Sandra and whoever she had. A foursome. Brilliant.'

'How old are you, Betty?'

'Twenty-two.'

'Sandra was a couple of years younger, wasn't she?'

'Yeah.'

'Whom did she have?'

'Lots.'

'But you had Rollo.'

Betty looked at her in silence for a moment and said, 'Yeah, I had Rollo.'

'There isn't much to do in a place like this, is there? I mean for people of your ages.'

Betty put her fingers to her temple and said, 'Let's see, there's bingo at the village hall, and country and western every summer in a wet field, and the young farmers' annual ball. Oh, yeah, lots and lots to do.'

The irony was heavy and Anne said, 'So you went to Kingstown?'

'Oh, great. Kingstown's a hole. No, Rollo, had a boat. We used to go down there or to London.'

'Did Mason ever go with you?'

'Mason?'

The way she said his name made it sound as though it was unfamiliar.

236

'Didn't he ever go with Sandra?'

'He came to Fontwell once. To the races.'

'Were they in love?'

Betty burst out laughing. 'Christ, no.'

'But they were having an affair.'

'He thought he was, anyway.'

'Sandra wasn't serious?'

'Serious? You sound like Sandra's mum.' She mimicked Lily Benson's voice. 'Sandra, you must be serious . . . Sandra, you mustn't talk like that . . . Sandra, I want you to promise me you won't . . . Sandra, please don't do that . . .'

Anne felt a sudden tightening of her stomach. 'Was Sandra a problem?'

'Who for?'

'Her mother.'

'What d'you mean, a problem?'

'I wondered whether they got on well or whether they had their difficulties, like most parents and children.'

Betty contemplated this for a moment then said, 'I dunno, I never had parents.'

'Have you always lived with your grandmother?'

'You must be joking.'

'Where did you live, Betty? And won't you tell me about your parents?'

She stared at Anne. The fear – if it had been fear – was gone. 'I thought you came to talk about Mason. You been talking a lot about Sandra. Now me.'

'One last question about Sandra,' Anne said. 'You've told me she was younger than you and she was therefore younger than Rollo and a lot younger than Mason. Doesn't that seem a bit odd? I mean Sandra was younger than you, her friend, by two years which is quite a lot as far as experience is concerned.'

Betty laughed. 'Experience? Sandra could teach me things and—'

There was the noise of a car engine and Betty turned her head to listen. 'You better go,' she said. 'That'll be Mitch. He doesn't like people coming here and asking questions. Go out the front.'

Anne left by the front passage. As she opened the door she heard a man's voice in the kitchen saying, 'Who the fuck's here?'

Betty said something she could not hear. She held the door open for another second and heard the man say, 'I found some bloody nigger down by the river and—'

Anne closed the door and went to her car.

22

It was incredible, Anne thought, when she looked at Beanie, that only a few months before she had been paralysed in the back legs. Seeing her, in her own place, in Tom's house, made this more immediate and she recalled with pleasure how much Hilly had done to bring the little dog back to her present feisty self. There was a big fire blazing in the open stove but the wooden house, which was more like a Bavarian shooting lodge than a dwelling in England, was, she thought, a gloomy place. The walls, lined in tongue-and-groove panelling, absorbed the light and even with the fire, it was still not cheerful.

Tom was kneeling in front of the fire with Hilly and Beanie. The dog was more interested in a plate of crumpets that were about to be toasted than in any of the human beings.

'Okay,' Tom said to Hilly, 'you've got it on the end of a fork, now don't push it too far towards the flames.'

Hilly extended the toasting fork with the crumpet towards the fire.

'Right,' said Tom, 'I'll do mine and your mother's.'

For Anne it was almost heart-stopping to watch them. This is where Paul should have been. Then she caught herself: *Don't think like that.*

They ate the toasted crumpets with farm butter and honey in the comb. Hilly said, 'Grandpa never makes teas like this.'

When they'd finished she and Beanie went outside to play and Tom said to Anne, 'There you are. Did I beat Hilly? Was I nasty to her?'

She smiled and shook her head. 'I hope I'm not going to have to pay for those remarks for too long.' Then she said, 'I went out to see a girl called Betty Sugden this afternoon. She was a friend of Sandra's.' She saw Tom frown. 'It's all part of Mason's background – and important now that he's gone silent again.'

'He's been like that all bloody day,' Tom said.

She'd got back from her visit to Betty and found Mason in his catatonic state, but now there was a reason for it. Someone had given him a newspaper with the story about the murder of Harold Taylor, the man who had confessed to the killing for which Jameson had been convicted. She'd sat with him for nearly an hour, talking softly about inconsequential things to try and bring him out of his state, but he had lain there, knees to his chest, his back to her, and had not recognised her presence.

Afterwards Tom had suggested that she should fetch Hilly and he'd give them a late tea.

'So what did you find out from Betty Sugden?' he said.

240

'The main thing is that the real Sandra Benson isn't the sweet, innocent young girl we heard about in court.'

'In what way?'

'She and Betty grew up together and went to school together. I'm not sure when their relationship started – it couldn't have been when they were small because there's a two-year age difference – but by the time they reached their late teenage years they seemed to have become a pair of swingers.'

'That's a nice old-fashioned word.'

She smiled. 'The problem really for these two young girls was the village. It was a typical village with village concerns but if you sit watching TV all day, as they seem to have done and as Betty's doing now, you have a wider horizon and expectations. And certainly Stepton doesn't fulfil them.'

'Sandra's father was a naval officer, wasn't he?'

'He'd come up through the ranks. Betty's father was a farm-hand. But the interesting thing as far as Mason's concerned is that he said in court that he was having an affair with Sandra and seems to have thought he was the only one. But if you listen to Betty, Sandra was playing the field.'

'I read the trial reports in detail,' Tom said. 'And I'm damned if I can remember a Betty Sugden, or any friend of Sandra's, for that matter, giving evidence.'

'I wondered about Betty too. I don't even recall seeing her in court. When I asked her why she hadn't told someone about Mason and Sandra having an affair she said she was away. I checked with the police and apparently she was serving time in the women's prison in Southgate for shoplifting.'

'Talking of checking up, Holroyd gave me some good news about Sophie Lennox. I'd always assumed that when people work for a TV company they have a job in the sense that you and I have jobs. But in television most of them are freelance. They're taken on for one series and when that contract ends in three months or six months, they're out, and looking for work. So they've all got ideas of their own for programmes which they try to develop for presentation to a production company. Obviously this is what inspired Sophie Lennox to work on a prison series. But according to Holroyd, she's landed a job on a consumer programme, which means that the prison one will be on hold until that contract ends. With luck, the idea might simply evaporate. Anyway, you're not to worry any more about her.'

'I'm very grateful.'

He dismissed this with a wave of his hand. 'A TV documentary-maker only has to ask a question to have us all running about like scalded cats. But it's over.'

'Unless Mason's behaviour brings it back.'

'We'll just have to see it doesn't.'

He got up from the floor and crossed the big double room to where the tea things were laid out. 'Another cup?'

'No thanks.'

She was staring at the fire seeing images in the burning wood. In the distance she could hear Hilly and Beanie. Tom came back and stood on one side of the stove. 'This is how families live all the time, you know. Not just once a month,' he said.

She sat forward. 'I think we must go.'

'Nonsense. It's early yet.'

'My father and Watch are doing strange things with bones.'

'You're changing the subject.'

'Yes, I am.'

'You know, one day we're going to – oh hell, forget it. Why don't we have dinner some time this week? London if you like. I've got an urge to spend money on good food.'

She turned her head away. Like most mothers she had been listening subconsciously to Hilly shouting. Now she was hearing nothing. She rose and went to the window. Hilly and Beanie usually played on the verandah or just down the steps in front of it. They weren't there. She craned one way, then the other, and saw a small car parked at the far corner of the house. Hilly was standing at the front window.

'Someone's here,' she said.

He went to the door, looked out and said, 'Oh Christ, it's Steffie.'

Anne was about to run but stopped herself and walked quickly along the outside verandah. Tom kept pace with her. Hilly was looking into the car and laughing. Anne could see Stephanie's dark hair and white face smiling from the driver's seat.

Stephanie looked up at them and said, 'Hello there, I've been talking to Hilly. Anne, you've got such a lovely little girl.' She turned to Hilly, 'I told you that, didn't I.'

'Yes,' Hilly said.

'Oh, Anne, she *is* lovely. You *are* lucky. Don't you think she's lucky, Tom?'

'Very lucky. What can I do for you?'

'Do?' Stephanie laughed. 'I was in Kingstown, I came to say hello.'

Anne heard her tone in amazement. There was not the slightest hint of the rage and bitterness of the telephone call from Wales.

'And to give you your mother's love,' Stephanie said. 'You know Roberto is there?'

'Yes, Mother told me he was coming.'

Anne stepped forward and lifted Hilly up, then walked back along the verandah. Opposite the front door she put her down. 'We're going now, darling.'

'Why?' Hilly said. 'She's a nice lady.'

Tom caught up with them. 'Please don't go.'

Anne held Hilly with one hand and turned towards him. She said in a soft but biting voice,

'Keep her away from me. And keep her away from Hilly.'

She took Hilly's hand, went to her car and drove away across the bumpy track towards the main road.

'Come on, old man,' Henry said to Watch. 'What about some scrambled eggs. You used to like scrambled eggs.'

'I'm not hungry, Judge.'

'You'll just fade away and we don't want that.'

'I had a toasted teacake at Mrs Benson's.'

Watch had had three toasted teacakes but Henry decided not to press for accuracy.

'That's not a proper meal.'

'I am going to have eh-bath.'

'That's the ticket, you go and have a bath and then we'll have a drink together.'

As Watch disappeared into his room, Henry heard Anne and Hilly arrive and went upstairs.

'You look very fierce,' he said to Anne after Hilly had gone to her room.

'Do I?'

'Anything I should know about?'

'Not really. It's just something that happened today.'

She poured them each a drink. It wasn't often that she drank whisky and Henry was surprised. But he had begun to learn how to live with his daughter and instead of questioning her he sat down and said, 'Well, do you want to hear my day?'

'What? Oh yes, you and Watch went to Stepton, didn't you?'

'And we took Mrs Benson out onto the search area. I think she started off thinking she was going to be kidnapped and sold into the white slave trade but she soon settled down.'

'Don't you think you're making her life untenable?'

'Can you think of anything more untenable than what she was enduring? Anyway she became much less suspicious and guarded. We really got on quite well. I think we cheered her up and raised her spirits. So much so that she didn't stop talking. About Sandra mostly. What a wonderful girl she was and how she, Mrs Benson, had not done her best for her . . . etc . . . etc . . . You can imagine the rest.'

'I've heard it. There is another side.'

'Of course there is. No one could be that perfect. Anyway, she gave Watch a handkerchief which she said had belonged to Sandra but poor old Watch marched all about the countryside with it in his hand and when nothing seemed to move him or whatever the phrase is she told us she wasn't exactly certain whether it was Sandra's handkerchief. It had been found in the search area – or I should say was alleged to have been found there – by a chap called Mitchell. And this creature arrived on the scene and was rude to Watch and to me and to her.'

'I was at his house about the same time.' Anne described what had happened.

'They do get around don't they, these people? And Watch was pretty sure we were being spied on by someone up on the Downs but we couldn't see anyone. The point was that Mitchell's arrival sort of upset Watch and he didn't want to go on with the search so Mrs Benson asked us back to her house and gave us tea. That's when she told us about her doubts that the handkerchief was her daughter's. I thought Watch was going to ask if he could see her daughter's room and I was glad he didn't. But just before we left she told Watch that she had something which she knew was Sandra's and next time she would bring it out and let Mr Watchman hold it, that's if Mr Watchman would like to.'

'She calls him Mr Watchman?'

'I think he rather likes it.'

Anne said, 'The more I go into this the more desperate I feel for that poor woman. What if she finds out that her daughter wasn't what she thought she was?'

'A trial is supposed to get at the truth,' Henry said.

'In Mason's case, I wonder if it ever will.'

It's not your handkerchief, my love. Mr Watchman got nothing from it. I know that isn't positive, but it's what I believe.

247

And did you know that Betty was living with Mitchell? Olive told me, and she should know. I don't know how she could. He's a dreadful man and he smells of the stables. He was so rude to us when we were looking for you. It's because I'm not giving him any money, I suppose.

Lily isn't sitting on her chair but standing by the window staring out into the gloaming. Is there dust on the glass? She'll have to clean it soon. And the kitchen cooker.

She is getting tired of cleaning.

And then they came back for a cup of tea and Mr Watchman had teacakes. He seems to like them. When we were having tea the phone rang and it was Peter. He said could I come to the pub and I had to say that I had visitors and he sounded, well, surprised.

Lily traces a little figure in the dust on the glass. She glances at her watch.

I'll go now, my love . . . I'll talk to you later.

She goes downstairs and looks at the cooker. It seems clean enough. You could overdo things like cleaning.

23

The house was on the outskirts of a village a few miles from Stepton. It was a small, brick-built bungalow that stood in the middle of a fair-sized garden. Anne rang the bell and a voice called, 'I'm at the back. Walk round.'

A woman with a spade in her hands came across a small lawn to meet her.

'I'm Mavis Timmins,' she said when Anne had introduced herself.

The day was fitfully sunny but the air was chill. Mrs Timmins seemed to live in a different, subtropical world. She was in her seventies and was wearing a short-sleeved shirt, thin trousers and black rubber boots up to her knees. She had a round face with long, grey hair pulled back into a pony-tail. Her skin was leathery and brown.

She slammed the spade into the newly turned earth and said, 'I love a bit of digging, don't you? People don't dig any more, they have machines to do it or hire men. I dig and I chop firewood. Now there's exercise. Nothing like a good bit of chopping. Let's take a seat.'

They sat in white garden chairs. Anne had not dressed for sitting outside and felt cold. Mrs

Timmins seemed impervious to weather. There were bulbs everywhere and a small apple tree was about to burst into blossom. It was the most crowded garden Anne had ever seen. There were little paved areas, trellises, urns, flower beds, vines – every inch had been cultivated or decorated, or both.

Mrs Timmins said, 'My daughter mentioned you wanted to talk about Stepton in the old days.'

'Did she tell you why?'

'She said you were from the prison where Mason Chitty is.'

'You knew him, I imagine.'

'Only as a little boy. I left Stepton when I got married and that was nearly forty years ago.' She glanced sideways at the spade and Anne had a feeling that she wanted to get up and give the rest of the patch a good going over. If she asked the question she'd come to ask and Mrs Timmins was still thinking about the pleasures of digging or chopping, it might be a wasted trip, so she eased into the subject.

'It must have been a very different place then.'

'Very. There weren't so many people. I went there the other day with my daughter Cindy and we had a drink at the Mayfly and it was packed and I asked the publican were they all visitors and he said no they all lived there and went to work in London every day. Forty years ago it used to be a proper village. People lived and worked there or on the farms. There was a grocer's shop and a

250

butcher and a baker and a shoemaker – not quite a candlestick maker – but there was an ironmonger's, oh everything. Nowadays there's just one little shop.'

'I've only met a few people here,' Anne said. 'The shopkeeper was one. And I met Kenny and his mother.'

'Oh, Kenny. He was also a little boy when I left.'

'And Mrs Drayton.'

'I used to go up to the big house quite often. They had a large staff in those days. Four or five in the house, three in the garden and all the farm labourers. And they had families so there was always something wrong with somebody. I know I was only a district nurse but really we were more like doctors then. I mean, you didn't just send everyone off to hospital. You tried to put things right yourself.'

'When I was up at the house I didn't see a servant or a gardener and I was told she'd sold a lot of her land to the Chittys.'

Mrs Timmins looked appalled. 'The old general would have had apoplexy if he'd been alive!'

'Who was he?'

'Elizabeth Drayton's father. General Humphrey Hastings. Hastings was her name before she married Dominic Drayton. They've been an Army family for a long time.'

'Not now. Her son Rollo went into the Air Force.'

'I never knew him. I've heard about him, of

course. Who hasn't? He was a ladies' man if there ever was one.'

She glanced hungrily again at the spade and Anne said quickly, 'You must have known Kenny's mother.'

'Of course I did. I practically delivered Kenny.'

'She said something strange to me. I asked whether she thought Mason could have killed Sandra Benson and she said you never knew what someone would do who started off life as a girl.'

Mrs Timmins straightened her back and twined the fingers of her rough hands. 'She said that?'

'Not in those exact words but that's the sense of it.'

'I'm surprised. It's not the sort of thing she would usually say to a stranger. She must have said it to tease you. I assume she didn't explain.'

'That's why I've come to you.'

'It's not something I talk about because I wouldn't want a libel action on my hands.'

'You can be absolutely sure that whatever you tell me here will be between the two of us.'

'Oh, it's all so long ago I don't know why I'm making such a fuss about keeping it secret. But whether it'll help Mason I don't know.'

'Anything might help.'

'Well, it's just a bit of mystery. It all goes back to that terrible winter when Mason was born. You've got to remember that in those days many more women had their children at home than they do now. At that time there were two women in Stepton who were pregnant, Kenny's mother, and Mrs Chitty. I'd seen them and they were both all right. I was specially glad about Mrs Chitty because as you know she lives very remotely. We thought we'd organised everything to the last detail but births won't be organised. A few days before Mrs Chitty was due it began to snow and everything went wrong. The roads became blocked and the midwife couldn't get through. It was just terrible. I've never seen anything like it. Electricity cables down, phone lines down. There were no proper snow ploughs or anything like that then. I was worried stiff about Mrs Chitty. Then her husband phoned. He said they were all right. The Hastings family had taken them in. His wife had given birth to a little girl and everything was fine.'

'A little girl?'

'That's what he said. I remember I was just on my way to check on Mrs Elkins when the call came and I told her about Mrs Chitty. She was about to have her baby and I remember she said she hoped hers was a girl too.'

'And?'

'The trouble was Mrs Elkins had a difficult birth. She was in labour for a long time, there was a delay in the second stage, and foetal distress. The doctor had to walk the last couple of miles to Stepton in gumboots. I was with Mrs Elkins for nearly forty-eight hours without a break. During that time the snow went on and on and there were huge winds and then suddenly the winds died and everything froze. So I set off to see Mrs Chitty and of course skidded on the ice. I ran my car off the road and spent the night in hospital. The following day I phoned the Hastings and they said we weren't to worry. Everything was fine and Elizabeth Hastings, as she was then, said she had a nurse there anyway. Well, the wind came up again only this time it was a south-westerly and the snow melted and the Chittys were able to get back to their own house.'

She paused and picked at a piece of hard skin on her hand. 'The point is that when I did go to check on Mrs Chitty the baby wasn't a girl but a little boy. I was as sure as I'm sitting here that Mr Chitty had said it was a girl but when I told him that's what I thought he'd said he replied no, it must have been a bad line. I suppose it might have been but there was something else. Mason, for that's who he became, looked to me a little older than a newly born baby should look. But even that's not unusual because every baby is different and some look older than others. But the two things . . . Well, I don't know.'

'What about the registration of birth?'

'I checked that. It wasn't any of my business really but I was so sure of what he'd said that I did eventually go and check the register. And there was only a baby boy called Mason born in Stepton on that day.'

254

'But you still think . . .?'

'I really don't know what to think. It was some time later that I remembered something else Mr Chitty had said on the phone to me: "We'll have to think of a name for her." He had said "her". I remember that as clearly as if it had happened yesterday.'

When Anne left Mrs Timmins she phoned the prison from her car and asked for Les Foley.

'I'm ringing to check on Mason Chitty,' she said.

'Nothing to report, doc, he's just the same as he was. His eyes are open but he's totally unresponsive.'

'I'm going out to Stepton and I'll be back at lunchtime. Would you tell Dr Melville?'

'He's not here. He had to go to Kingstown General.'

As far as she knew there were no patients on transfer either one way or the other. 'Trouble?' she said.

'It's Mrs Melville.'

She'd never thought of Fanny Fielder as Mrs Melville but thought of her now and her foolhardy rejection of sticks and crutches. 'I didn't know she'd come from Wales. Was it a fall?'

'Not Dr Melville's mother,' Foley said. 'His exwife. She OD'd.'

'Oh, my God! When?'

'Last night, I think.'

'Is she still alive?'

'I don't know.'

She drove to the hospital. She had been feeling angry with herself and guilt-ridden since her outburst at Tom's house. She saw him come out of the main entrance and walk towards the staff car-park. She watched him as he drew nearer. He was unshaven and his thin face looked even thinner.

He saw her waving, crossed to her car and got in beside her.

'Les told me,' she said.

'The Castle Hotel phoned me early this morning.'

'God, I'm sorry. How is she?'

'She'll be all right.'

'Well, that's something. And, Tom, I'm desperately sorry for what I said to you. I was going to take you for a drink this evening and go down on my knees.'

He waved his hand dismissively in a characteristic gesture.

'No, I mean it,' she said. 'I was stupid. It's not your fault she's like she is. Just as I suppose it's not my fault my father is as he is. Yet one feels responsible.'

'From what I know of your father the two things don't bear any comparison.'

'Do you know what happened?'

'The usual. She's done it before. Mogadon and a quarter bottle of whisky. They only found her because she tried to phone me about four in the

256

morning and asked the desk to put through the call. Apparently she sounded so bloody odd that they went up to her room.'

'I didn't realise she was staying at the hotel.'

'I went round there last night. I thought after what had happened and after what she'd said on the phone to you that I'd get tough with her. I told her there was no chance of us ever getting back together. And I told her to lay off you and my mother. In fact to leave us all alone. She was like she was when you were out at my house with Hilly – agreeing and being sweet reasonableness and saying yes that was the best thing and how sorry she was that she'd bothered us all. I should have known.'

'Do you have to go through the desk at the hotel if you're making a phone call? I stayed there when we had some alterations done to the house. I'm sure it's direct dialling.'

'It is. It was her way of letting us know what she was in the process of doing.'

Anne felt even worse than she had and when he said, 'I know it's early but I need a drink,' she drove him to their pub. He had a double vodka and she had coffee.

'What's going to happen now?' she said.

'About Steffie? God knows. Do you mind if we don't talk about her?'

'Of course not.'

'What have you been up to?'

She told him about Mrs Timmins. 'That's fascinating,' he said, 'but it doesn't really get us much further. And I wonder if she isn't just remembering what she *thought* had happened. Her daughter said her memory wasn't what it was.'

The way he spoke made her realise that he wasn't able to concentrate on anything else but Stephanie for the moment.

She said, 'I'd like to go on out to Stepton. There is some unfinished business there.'

He nodded briefly. 'I'll be at the nick. I don't want to go home and I don't want to be sitting around Kingstown General.'

'You said something about going out to dinner.'

He looked at her in amazement and she said hastily. 'That was a crass way to put it. I simply meant that with Stephanie in the state she's in, you mustn't be away from Kingstown and I was going to say, why not come round and have that dinner with me at home? You'll be near a phone and only a mile away from Kingstown General if anything should happen. In fact if you wanted a bed there's a spare room.'

He slapped one hand on top of the other. 'Done and done!' he said. 'That's the best offer I've had for a long time.'

24

Stepton House in the bright sunlight of a spring day was showing its age and neglect. The first time Anne had seen it was on a dull and rainswept evening, but now the light was unforgiving. There were areas where roof tiles had blown away, the painted window frames and door bubbled with wet rot, weeds were growing in the driveway and the big steps going up to the front door were green with moss.

Anne pulled at the bell and heard, deep inside the house, its dismal ringing. No one came. She rang again. A car stood just below the steps, one of its front doors slightly open. Lights were on in a downstairs room. As she had at Mrs Timmins, she walked to the rear of the house. The back door was open, leading into the big kitchen and scullery. Here too, in spite of the bright daylight, the lights were on.

She put her head round the door and called, 'Anyone in?' There was no reply. 'Hello!' She went into the kitchen. 'Mrs Drayton!'

She moved out of the kitchen into the passage and put her head into the living-room. It was empty. She crossed the passage to the other side of the

house, passed a dining-room with a long oak
refectory table, went into an inner hallway and then
to the small sitting-room. The door was ajar and
she could smell woodsmoke from the fire.

She knocked. 'Mrs Drayton?'

The room was dark, the curtains drawn. A log
was smouldering in the big fireplace. There was a
TV in the corner, a large chesterfield and a couple
of leather armchairs. There was a figure lying on
the chesterfield and as Anne entered the room the
figure rose. 'What the hell are you doing in my
house?' it said.

In a white night-dress and an old red dressing-
gown, Mrs Drayton reminded Anne of Miss
Havisham. There was a pillow on the chesterfield
and Anne realised she had been sleeping there. On
a small table in front of her was a half-empty bottle
of whisky and a glass.

'I'm sorry to disturb you,' Anne said.

'What is it?'

'I'd like to talk to you.'

'You've no right to come into a private house.'
Her voice was slurred and thick with sleep.

'I rang at the door several times and then went
round to the back.'

Mrs Drayton poured herself some whisky and
drained it. 'Well?' she said.

'Would you mind if I sat down?'

She was very different from the woman Anne
had met when she had come to look at Watch's

bleeding nose. The elegance was gone, the hauteur now merely ludicrous. She poured herself another drink and sat in one of the chairs by the fire. Her head was turned away from Anne and she sipped the whisky, letting it roll around her mouth before swallowing it. Her hair, which was one of her most attractive features and which was usually a silver mane combed back, hung about her face.

'Well?' she said again.

'I've been talking to several people and I thought I'd check with you some of the things they told me.'

She did not react and Anne said, 'Does the name Mavis Timmins mean anything to you?'

'Should it?'

'I wondered.'

'No, it doesn't.'

'She was the district nurse here more than forty years ago.'

'So?'

'There was a very bad winter. She told me a story of that time which has special reference to Mason Chitty and it concerns you.'

'I don't see how I could be involved with Mason Chitty.'

Anne described how she had gone to see Mrs Timmins and what she'd been told about the winter when Mrs Chitty was pregnant. Elizabeth poured herself a little more whisky and stared down at the liquid in the glass.

'I remember that,' she said. 'It was bad for a few

days. I suppose I remember it because we had the Chitty family here.'

Her voice was stronger but her pronunciation had become more slurred and Anne wondered how long she'd been drinking. It was now two o'clock in the afternoon. She might have been drinking for most of the night and gone to sleep in the early morning.

Elizabeth said, 'People like the Chittys lived rough in those days. I don't think they had a phone, and I'm sure they didn't have a bathroom. I remember the house as being one of the coldest I've ever been in.'

'Not a good place to be when you're about to give birth,' Anne said.

'Certainly not when the snow is falling.'

'So you took them in?'

'Her husband brought her down the two miles from their place, through the snow, and asked if we would. We were cut off from the village too, but at least we had a warm house.'

'And servants to look after them.'

'No, the house servants were in London to prepare for my father's arrival.'

'And that's where Mason was born, in your house? Was it an easy birth?'

'No births are easy. You've got a child, you should know.'

'Who delivered it? The nurse?'

'What nurse?'

'Mrs Timmins said that when she spoke to you on the phone you told her she wasn't to worry about anything, that the baby was born, that it was fine and so was Mrs Chitty. She remembers you saying you had a nurse there, otherwise she would have come in spite of the weather.'

'I don't see how I could have said that.'

'Were you alone then?'

'My sister Margaret was with me. She'd been staying at the London house, then my father wrote that he was coming back on leave, so she came here. He was with the British Army of the Rhine in Germany.' She pronounced the words with difficulty.

'Weren't you afraid of what might happen?'

'Of course we were. But what were we supposed to do? There was another woman in labour in the village and the only doctor had to come from Kingstown.'

'So you spoke to the district nurse and told her everything was all right?'

'Well, it *was* all right.'

'Even without a nurse?'

'Why do you go on about that?'

'Mrs Timmins seems to have misunderstood the telephone calls.'

Elizabeth rose, walked unsteadily to the fire-place, and pushed at the big log. Flames sputtered briefly, then died, and some of the smoke rolled into the room. She turned. 'You keep on mentioning this woman whom I can't recall ever meeting.'

'I think you probably did. She said she came up here quite often to patch up the servants.'

'Perhaps she did. I don't suppose you want a drink?'

'No, thank you.'

'Do you think I'm an alcoholic?'

'Mrs Drayton, I have no opinion.'

'Well, I'm not. Not yet anyway. But there are times . . . Yesterday was Rollo's birthday. I always gave him a good present. The year before he died I gave him a Purdey. Do you know what a Purdey is, Dr Vernon?'

'I'm afraid I don't.'

'The finest shotgun in the world. I don't think he ever had chance to use it. The Gulf War came along.'

'Could we just go back to Mrs Timmins for the moment?'

'I'm sick of talking about that bloody woman! Can't we talk about something else?' She went to the window and flung back the curtains. The bright sunlight caused her to flinch and cover her eyes. Her movements were like her speech; slurred.

'It won't take a minute,' Anne said.

'Must have another drink then. That's what Dommie always said when anything came up that bored him or disconcerted him. It was funny really. I mean he was so bloody frightened of my father before we were married that he always had another drink or two before coming to the house. That's what the Army does to you. Dommie was a major which I suppose isn't much really. Father was a general and by God he let you know it.'

'Just to get back to Mrs Timmins for a moment . . .'

'Oh Christ, all right, Mrs Bloody Timmins.'

'She told me in detail what happened and I was surprised she remembered so much. She had to remain at Mrs Elkins's house because she was having difficulty in her labour but she says she spoke not only to you but to Mr Chitty. I think he phoned her from here just after his wife had given birth. It was to say that she mustn't worry, everything was fine. Don't you think that's an odd thing to do?'

'What's odd about it?'

'You said yourself that there's no such thing as an easy birth. I think I would have wanted the doctor, or at least the district nurse, to come and examine me, wouldn't you?'

'I don't know what the hell you're getting at. She was all right and so was the baby.'

'How did you know? Had you ever helped at a birth before? Mrs Timmins was very worried. But then she was told that there was a nurse here, so she was less worried. But there wasn't a nurse, was there?'

'Who the hell do you think you are? You're not a

detective, you're not a lawyer and you come here asking—'

'I'm a doctor, one of those people with a right to ask certain questions. You don't have to answer me but I have the right. Now there's something else.'

'I don't want to go on.'

'Have another drink, isn't that what you do, like your husband?'

'Oh shit!'

'Mrs Timmins remembers other things.'

'She must have a marvellous memory, that's all I can say.'

Anne noticed a change in her voice, it was still slurred but the stridency had gone.

'She says that when she spoke to Mr Chitty he referred to the baby as a girl. He said *she* was fine and that they'd have to find a name for *her*. But when she got up to the Chittys' house after a few days the baby was a boy. And he denied ever having said it was a girl.'

'She's talking rubbish! Absolute rubbish! The baby was a boy, of course it was a boy.'

'She isn't the only one who mentioned this to me. Someone in the village said so too.'

'You know what villages are like.'

'I'm afraid I don't. I came down from London.'

'Any bloody thing gets exaggerated and passed on. Specially if it's got to do with, well, the landowner.'

'But this didn't have anything to do with what

you call the landowner, did it? I mean, it had to do with the Chittys unless . . .'

'You go on and on! I'm sick of it.' She was silent for a moment then she said, 'Anyway, no one said anything to me.'

'Of course not. You're the local *grande dame*.'

'You can't hide things in a village. People find out things. Interesting things . . . nasty things . . . scandalous things . . . and they want to share them . . .' Her voice had drifted away as though she was talking to herself. 'And who're you going to share them with if not a neighbour? A tells B and says keep it to yourself. B tells C and says it's a secret between the two of them . . .'

Anne said, 'Whose baby was it, Mrs Drayton? Yours?'

She looked up angrily and then, abruptly, seemed to collapse, not in any dramatic exterior way but Anne sensed that she was simply breaking down inside. She said nothing for a while, then slowly shook her head. 'Oh no . . . no . . . no . . . Not mine. I'd never have let Harry Chitty bed me. No, it was my sister Maggie's. She'd fancied him, lots of women had, and he'd got her pregnant . . . Well, Chitty had no money for an abortion. In those days there was no such thing as a legal abortion. And we didn't know how to go about a thing like that. We were as innocent as new-born lambs . . . Of course there was gin and hot baths and that sort of thing. She tried all those and they didn't work. So

I went with her to London and we got off the train at Waterloo and asked a taxi driver if he knew of anyone who would remove a baby and he said if we didn't clear off he'd call the police. We were pathetic.'

'Couldn't she have kept it?'

'It was a different type of society then. No one of our class could keep a child born out of wedlock. Specially not if the girl had been tupped by someone like Harry Chitty. And even more specially . . . not girls like Maggie and me who had a father like the General. God what a shit he was!'

There was a pause. Anne opened her mouth to ask a question, then decided not to speak at all. Slowly, Elizabeth began to talk again, this time so softly that Anne could hardly hear her.

'There's a tycoon in Australia who, when he was a little boy starting his Christmas holidays, was forced by his father to go back a thousand miles by himself to fetch a tennis racquet he'd forgotten to bring home from school. My father would have applauded that. We were in the Scottish Highlands on holiday once and Margaret wet her bed. She must have been about seven. We'd only just got there, but he sent us home. My mother took us. She was frightened sick of him. We were all frightened sick of him really. He stayed on to fish the Spey.'

'What happened about the baby?'

'Maggie had just had hers. She was staying in

the London house by herself and then father said
he was coming back to London on leave. He never
liked to come down here in the winter, so she
brought the baby here. She was absolutely terrified
of what he would do if he found out. So when Mrs
Chitty's baby girl died soon after being born I said,
why not let her bring up Margaret's? I mean, it
would be with its real father, anyway. We'd pay.
Mother was dead by that time and we both had
money from her, so that wasn't a problem. And
that's what happened. We buried the poor little
dead baby and the Chittys went home with Mason.'

'And the nurse?'

'There wasn't a nurse. It was just something I
said to stop that woman coming up to the house.'

'You paid for his education?'

'And for his clothes. And after his father died we
had to give his mother an allowance.'

'Did Samuel know he was only a half-brother?'

'She may have told him. She hated Mason. I
suppose you can't blame her. She had no choice
and the money was good.' She paused, then said,
'So now you know. But if you try to use any of this
as evidence, I'll deny I ever said it.'

'What difference does it make to you now? Is it
your sister?'

'No, she died a long time ago.'

'Well, why?'

Mrs Drayton had tears in her eyes. The whisky
was doing its work. Anne thought she was literally

269

coming apart in front of her.

'I don't know,' she said.

'Don't you think you owe it to Mason?'

'Perhaps. But what do we owe to Lily? To the victim? That's what I keep asking myself.'

'Why Lily? Sandra was the victim.'

'There are ways of being victims and I only realised how badly we had treated Lily after Sandra died.'

'Is that why you've organised the search?'

'Yes. We're never going to find her. We know that. The Chittys have too much land to cover. She could be anywhere. And the others, I mean the other working parties, have largely given up. People get bored very quickly.'

'Why go on then, if you feel like that?'

Elizabeth paused again and then said, 'It's worth it because it shows Lily we care and it gives her something to occupy herself with. She's been bloody lonely and I know what that means.' She stood up. 'I want to show you something.'

Anne followed her upstairs and into a room on the first floor. There was a cricket bat in one corner and some old golf clubs. A Royal Air Force dress uniform hung on a hanger on the wall and an Air Force cap lay on the bed.

'This was Rollo's room,' Elizabeth said. 'All his clothes are still in the wardrobe and the drawers. I kept it like this just as Lily Benson keeps Sandra's room. I kept it for quite a long time after I knew he wasn't coming back. Then I thought I'd clear it. But I never have and now I suppose I never will. He was a wonderful child; kind and generous and with the most wonderful manners. He used to look after me like a brother.' She picked up the cap, looked at it, and threw it back on the bed. 'Isn't it a pity they have to grow up?'

Anne saw a look of total misery in her eyes.

When Anne got back to the prison that afternoon she felt dazed with tiredness, but she went through to see Mason.

'Hello,' she said. 'How are you today?'

He was curled up, knees to chest, staring at the wall.

'I know you don't feel like talking but I thought I'd tell you that I went to Stepton today. I talked to Mrs Drayton, and I've also talked to Betty. Mrs Drayton told me a lot about your background, Mason.'

He did not indicate that he had heard her and she said, 'Now I know who you really are and it tells me much more about you than I knew before. When you feel like it, I think we should have a talk.'

She went back to her office and found a note from Tom on her desk. 'I've gone to the hospital,' it read. 'She's not out of danger yet but the prognosis is good. I'd love to take you up on your offer for tonight.'

She had been so wrapped up in Mason's past

that she had forgotten her offer. If she was going to feed Tom she would need to shop and there was also the spare room to prepare. She thought of phoning her father and asking him to start on these two jobs, then instantly dismissed the thought as lunacy.

25

It was as well that Anne had dismissed the idea of involving her father for when she got home, an excited Hilly met her at the door. 'Mr Watch is very sick,' she said in a loud whisper.

'Not *very*,' her grandfather said coming up behind her.

'You *said* very.' Hilly was indignant.

'No I didn't. I said *rather*, which doesn't mean the same thing at all.'

'Well, is he or isn't he?' Anne put the carrier bag down on the kitchen table.

'He threw up,' Henry said.

'He was *sick*!' Hilly said.

'Any idea why?' Anne said.

'I think it's just reaction. He's stressful from what happened to him in Maseru with the hotel cook. And then the flight and—'

'And getting mixed up with the Sandra Benson murder. I told you not to let him.'

'And what he had for lunch,' Hilly said. 'Uuuuuugh.'

'What did he have for lunch?' Anne said.

Henry paused. 'Well, I thought I'd give him something really good out of my little cookbook—'

'What?'

'I can't just recall the name but it was pork – and stuffing of a sort. Leg of pork stuffed with sausage meat. But I thought that leg of pork was a bit on the hefty side just for the two of us since neither you nor Hilly seem to relish my cooking these days. So I bought a shoulder. Didn't really fancy sausage meat in it but you know how I like paté. And that's all minced up too.'

'My God, you didn't stuff pork with paté, did you?'

'I can't think why you're adopting that tone.'

'But the richness! No wonder he was sick!'

'Rubbish. It's got nothing to do with that. He eats pork pies at pubs and they can't be good for you.'

'Should I see him?'

'Examine him?' Henry's voice was horrified.

'You know I'd never do that,' Anne said. 'No, I'd just go and say hello and see how he is.'

'Watch wouldn't like a woman near him at a time like this.'

'Well, he's your responsibility.'

'Right. That's settled that.'

She started to unpack the groceries. 'Tom's coming to stay the night. His ex-wife OD'd and she's in hospital but is going to be all right he thinks. It'll be easier for him to stay in town in case he's needed.'

'OD'd! What sort of language is that? Most of the folk in Lesotho speak better English. There's some of the pork left over if you want it for Tom.'

'I don't think so, I've got nothing against him.'

'Highly amusing.'

The phone rang. It was Les Foley.

'It's about Mason Chitty,' he said.

'My God, not again!' Anne said.

'No doc, nothing's wrong, not that I can see anyway. It's just that he's started to talk again and he wants to see you. Says it's urgent.'

'Can't it wait until morning or can't he talk to someone else?'

'He's very fragile. Says what he's got to tell you is important. He wants you, doc.'

'Okay. I'll come in later. Tell him I'll be there in a couple of hours.'

'He wants you now, doc.' She felt the pressure in his tone.'

'What do you think, Les?'

'I think you should, if you don't mind me saying so.'

'All right, I'll be there in a few minutes.' She looked at her watch. 'And you should be on your way home, so don't wait for me. But warn Security that I'm coming in.'

She went back to the kitchen and told her father the news. 'I don't know what you're going to do with Tom. Why don't you nip out and get some Chinese or Thai takeaways?'

'What a ghastly idea,' Henry said. 'Why not the pork?'

'If you give him the pork I'll never speak to you again. Okay?'

'Is that a threat or a promise?'

Mason was sitting on the edge of his bed in the bleak secure room. He was wearing his pyjamas and a light dressing-gown without a belt. She remembered the word Les Foley had used: fragile. It suited him. He'd lost weight and his hands and arms were thin and so was his face. He had that transparent look that very old people get, as though bones will snap easily.

'How are you feeling?' she said.

He did not reply and for a moment she found irritation rising. 'Look, Mason, Les Foley told me you wanted to see me urgently.'

He turned to face her. 'You didn't tell me,' he said.

'Didn't tell you what?'

'About the man who was murdered at The Hawes prison.'

'No, I didn't. It seemed you had enough to worry about without that. And remember, he'd confessed to killing a child and child-killers are always at risk in prison. But Sandra wasn't a child. I suppose I knew that eventually someone would show you the paper or tell you. But, Mason, people are killed in prison very, very rarely. And you aren't in his category. So please don't worry about it.'

'But you didn't want me to know and I must

know. I have to plan my life.'

'Of course, and I was going to tell you later. But you weren't communicating with us.'

'Why do you think that was?'

'Was it because I hadn't told you?' He didn't reply and she said, 'These silences have happened before and it wasn't the reason then. I think perhaps you're looking for an excuse.'

'I didn't feel like talking.'

'All right, let's leave that. What was it you wanted to tell me?'

'When you came in earlier you said you'd been to see people in Stepton. You said you'd talked to Mrs Drayton.'

'That's right.'

'She's a bloody cow.'

'Why do you say that?'

'Because she is. She and that rotten son of hers. And the rotten husband. And the rotten father.'

This was a new Mason, she thought. She hadn't heard him like this. It was as though he had gone into a long sleep and come out with a slightly changed personality.

'What did she tell you?' he said. 'Did she tell you about me?'

'Yes, she did.'

'What?'

'Just about everything, I think, or at least, everything she knew.'

He made a derisive sound with his lips.

277

'Why didn't you tell me, Mason?'

'Why should I? It's not something I'm proud of.'

'When did you know you were illegitimate?'

He looked down at his hands, then back at her. 'When I was about ten. It was soon after my father died and my mother – or adoptive mother, I should say – took me into a room and locked the door and told me I didn't belong to her and that the people I belonged to were dead. That I was an adopted child. Adopted *and* illegitimate. She said she was telling me because one day I'd find out and she wanted me to know before that so I'd be warned never to say anything. She made me promise. She made me swear on the Bible that I would never speak about it; not even to her and Samuel.'

'Did she tell you who your parents were?'

'She told me everything. She said my father was a terrible man and she was glad he was dead. And she told me my real mother had been killed in a riding accident. She told me they were sending me away to school and when I'd finished school I was to work on the farm.'

'Did you know she got an allowance for you?'

'I knew she couldn't have afforded to send me to boarding school.'

'She still gets the allowance.'

'I suppose that's to keep her mouth shut. If only they knew. She never tells anybody anything, not about our family.' He paused, then said, 'You said you'd spoken to Betty as well.'

'I wanted to find out about Sandra. To see if that might help you in any way.'

He got up, shook his head and said, 'What's it to you? Why do you care about helping me?'

'Because . . . well, lots of reasons, but I don't think you've had much help in the past, have you?' He didn't answer and she probed a little more deeply. 'Unless Sandra was supportive.'

He laughed grimly. 'Is that what Betty said?'

'I didn't get that impression.'

He went to the window and stood looking out at the small piece of lawn and the flowers which marked the hospital as different from the rest of the prison.

'Did you really think Betty would tell you anything that would help me?'

'I had to try her.'

He was silent for a long time, staring out of the window. His shoulders were slack and his arms hung down limply. He looked, she thought, like a man who was totally defeated by prison. It was a depressive condition she had seen many times.

'Do you want to know what happened to Sandra?' he said at last.

She felt a sudden chill. 'Do you know?'

'Oh, yes, I know. Do you want to hear? Do you really want to hear?'

'If you want to tell me.'

He began to speak in a rambling, unstructured narrative. She could see him going deeply into his

279

memory and getting lost there for short periods. Sometimes if he was silent she was silent too, at others, when she thought it was the way forward, she would prompt him and say, 'Go on, Mason.' And all the time she was aware of the great silence that hung over the hospital. The working day was over. They might have been the only ones there.

He started by talking about the village and as she listened she realised she was hearing about a place she didn't know. This was not the English village out of the tourist brochures.

At the centre of the narrative were Betty and Sandra, neither of whom had an entrée into old money or new money. At the other end of the social scale, they avoided what they called the CHTs. Anne had not heard that phrase before and had to have Mason explain that the letters stood for council house tenants.

'They were snobs, then?' she said.

'In their own way.'

Mason had watched both girls grow up. When Sandra was little he had befriended her.

'She didn't have any friends, not even Betty when she was small,' he said. 'There was something about her that didn't make friends easily.'

She had had a bike then and cycled along the gallops. That was how he had met her. The friendship then had been platonic.

'I wasn't a dirty old man,' he said. 'I wasn't a flasher in a raincoat. She used to cycle near the farm and we had a Shetland pony. I would saddle it up and let her ride. This was usually after school. Her mother was working as a secretary in Kingstown at that time and didn't get home till well after Sandra, so she had time on her hands.'

He began to walk slowly up and down the secure room as he spoke. 'I watched her grow up, and she grew up fast. By the time she was fifteen or sixteen she was mature, or at least she looked mature. And she and Betty and Rollo started going around together. You understand what I'm saying?'

'Yes, I think so.'

'I mean, here was a kid I'd known and she wasn't a kid any longer and things were starting to happen. I'm looking back now. I don't think I knew that then. It's hindsight. I thought we had something between us, you see. Because when she was about eighteen we were walking up on the Downs and she said would I like to kiss her? And I did. And she said she loved me.'

He stopped and sat on the bed as far away from Anne as he could. 'Does that sound silly?'

'Absolutely not. She'd known you for a long time. You'd done things together. Why shouldn't she say that?'

'She didn't mean she loved me like a daughter loves a father or a sister loves a brother.'

'I know what she meant. Girls of that age are often highly sexually motivated.'

'She said she loved me. That she'd always loved

me. She said I was the only one who'd been a friend to her. Can you imagine it? Me hearing things like that? And believing them, for Christ's sake!'

He wiped his mouth with the sleeve of his dressing-gown and said, 'Since I've been in prison I've had time to think. That's the one thing prison gives you: time. I've thought about Sandra and my relationship with her. I think you could say I became obsessed. And you know something? So did Samuel. He wanted her and I had her.' He rubbed at his mouth again.

'You all right, Mason?'

'It's all this talking. My mouth's bone dry.'

'You want some water?'

'What I really want is a couple of beers, but I could make do with a coffee.'

She went to the door and looked into the passageway. It was dark and empty. The health-care staff must be in the ward, she thought. She turned back and said, 'I'll make you a coffee. Come into my room and we can go on talking there.'

He followed her and she closed the door of her office and put on the kettle. 'How do you like it?'

'Milk and two, please.'

'You say your brother—'

'Half brother.'

'Sorry. You say he became obsessed too.'

'He always wanted what I had, not that I had much. Like the things I brought home from school. We played hockey there and he took my hockey

282

stick and smashed it against the wall of the stables. And he took my squash racquet and broke that. They didn't play hockey or squash at his school. These were "upper-class" games and he hated that. He hated the fact that I went to a decent school and he hated me. So when Sandra came for walks with me along the river or in the woods he'd sometimes follow us in the Land-Rover. He really wanted her. Probably because I had her. But she thought he was common as muck.'

'Did she know about your background? Did you ever tell her?'

'I was frightened at the very thought of telling people after what the old woman had made me swear. This is the first time I've talked about it and I'm still frightened.'

'You don't have to be, Mason. No one's going to harm you for talking.'

'That's what I said to myself. I thought if anyone would listen properly you would.'

He paused and to prompt him she said, 'It's not surprising, is it, that Samuel was jealous?'

'Sending me to a public school was my real mother's idea, I suppose. Perhaps to make up for the fact that she had abandoned me.'

'She never came to see you?'

'Never. Her father would have killed her if he'd found out.'

'And your aunt, Mrs Drayton?'

'She was a bloody snob. I saw her in the village

occasionally but it was as though we were just members of the same small community. When I was a child her father was still alive and everybody was frightened of him. So she wouldn't have said anything. And it stayed like that after he died – well, she was married then. Easier to leave things as they were.'

'Had your real mother married?'

'No, she was only in her twenties when it happened.'

Anne thought briefly of the complex web of secrecy that had been sown on that snowy winter's day and wondered how many others in Stepton had secrets. What was Kenny's mother's secret, what was Betty's grandmother's secret, Mitchell's secret, Lily Benson's, Elizabeth Drayton's? They would all have secrets of some sort but unless they were kept the village would disintegrate. You had to keep your mouth shut in a village like Stepton. It was self-preservation.

'Go on about Sandra,' she said.

'We became lovers.'

'Secret lovers, of course.'

'Of course. I suppose Samuel guessed. But Sandra wanted it kept secret. She didn't want her mother or anyone else in the village to know. Samuel was driving a taxi in Kingstown then and started to dabble in property, so he was away quite a bit. I never took her to the house because my . . . because Mrs Chitty was always there. So I made a place in the stables where we could go. I made it comfortable and clean. It was a good time for me. The best I've ever had. In some ways she was just a little girl, but looking back now I can see it was an act.'

'How was that?'

'Well, she used to say to me, Mason I've seen a lovely jersey or I've seen a ring or I've seen this or that. And I'd say let me get it for you. I really wanted to. I wanted to show how much I loved her. And she would say no, no, and I would get it and she would be pleased. But after a while I found she was doing that with others as well. She and Betty.'

'Men in the village?'

He finished his coffee and his voice was stronger. 'Rollo for one. They used to go down to his boat. And Mike Treagust. And Mitchell. And there were others. People from the next village, even men from Kingstown.'

'What you're saying is that Sandra and Betty were running a kind of prostitution racket in Stepton.'

Everyone was giving them something. Some little present. It wasn't a real racket. Not like in the brothels or the prostitutes on the streets. It was a kind of cottage industry.'

'And you found out? How?'

'Kenny.'

'Kenny?'

'He's not as stupid as you think he is or he likes

to pretend. I found out later that Kenny used to watch them doing it. What's the word for someone who does that?'

'You mean a voyeur?'

'Yeah, that's it. That's what Kenny was. Rollo caught him once and gave him a thrashing.'

'So Kenny told you about them?'

'He took me up the road to Mitchell's house. He was on his bike of course and I followed. It was night and you could see through a chink in the curtains. Mitchell and Betty, and Sandra and a man I didn't recognise. And they were . . . well, they were doing things. With the light on.'

'Do you think Kenny had watched you?'

'I doubt it.'

He went silent again and Anne said, 'So what did happen, Mason?'

'I killed her.'

'What did you say?'

'You said what happened next and I said I killed her.'

She felt as though she'd been struck over the heart.

'Mason, you've said all along that you were innocent. Now you say you're guilty. I don't know what to believe any more.'

'I'll tell you the way it happened then. It was a couple of days, maybe three or four, after Kenny had taken me to Mitchell's place and I'd seen her. She was naked and so was the other man. All four.

286

Christ, with the light on! I thought about it a lot. I didn't want to be wrong about her because we went so far back. Right to when she was a kid on the Shetland pony. So I thought, I'll forget what I saw and maybe she meant it when she said I was the one she really loved. Dear God, what a bloody idiot I was! To make it worse I wanted to give her a proper present — a big one — and I thought how happy she'd been as a kid when I'd taken her riding so I bought her a horse. A really beautiful gelding. I paid the bloody earth for it and I took Sandra up to the stables and I said I had a present for her because I wanted her to be mine and she said she was and I said well then she mustn't do what she'd been doing and she said what was that and I told her. She began to get angry so I showed her the horse and told her it was hers. You know what she did? She swore at me and said she didn't want a bloody horse. How about a car if I was thinking of transport? And I pleaded with her. I reminded her of what she'd said about loving me.'

Anne felt her heart go out to him.

He put his hands over his face, hiding his eyes, and then he said, 'Oh God . . . that was the beginning of it. Something seemed to turn over in my head. I remember calling her a whore. I remember telling her what I'd seen up at Mitchell's place. And she spat in my face. So I grabbed her. I didn't mean to harm her then. I just grabbed her. I think I tried to kiss her and she spat at me again.

Then I went kind of loony. We began to fight. And then I don't remember anything. I think she must have hit me with something.'

He paused. She could see that he was trembling. Finally he said, 'I hadn't meant to kill her. Never had any intention. But she fought, you see, and I fought back.'

'Mason, are you sure you want to tell me this? You know I can't keep it to myself.'

'I know and yes, I am.'

While he had been talking Anne's mind had been racing ahead of him. Nothing like this had happened to her in her short career in the prison service but one thing she knew: she had to have a witness to what he was saying. But it was now ED, evening duty. The governor would have left and so would the senior management.

'Just excuse me for a second, Mason.' She picked up the phone and got through to Security.

An officer answered and said, 'Sorry, doc, we've got an emergency. There's a fight in the remand wing.'

She replaced the phone and turned back to Mason. 'Would you repeat what you've just told me if I bring in a health-care officer?'

He thought for a moment and then said, 'All right.'

'I think there's one in the ward, I'll go and get him.'

She hurried out of her room and went into the

ward but the officer wasn't there. One of the patients told her that he had been cleaning up after another patient who had been sick. She ran to the kitchen area and heard someone turning on a tap in the recess. She called, 'Is that you, Frank?'

'Yes, doc.'

'I need you in my room urgently.'

'Be with you in a sec, doc. I'll just lock the ward.'

She went back to her room but Mason wasn't there. Assuming he had gone to his own room she went along the corridor but when she opened his door the room was empty.

'Oh God!' she said aloud and ran back to her office.

A shadow beyond her desk caught her eye. Mason was on the floor. He was on his knees, leaning forward like pictures she had seen of Japanese soldiers in the act of committing hara kiri.

And that's what he had done. He had committed hara kiri, not with a sword but with the cord of the venetian blinds.

Frank, the health-care duty officer, arrived.

'Help me!' she said.

Mason's weight had caused the cord to bite deeply into his neck. His breathing was raucous but she wasn't worried so much about that. What was worse was the fact that the cord was cutting off the blood supply to his brain.

They managed to lift his weight off the cord but it was too tight for their fingers to get underneath it.

'Get the security box!'

Frank ran from the room. In each wing of the prison and in the hospital there was a special tool, a pair of scissors with one blade turned and flattened so that it could slide under tight suicide cords and cut them like anvil secateurs.

'Hang on, Mason!' she said to the purple face.

She fought again to get her fingernails under the cord but Mason had twisted it round his neck several times and it had sunk a quarter of an inch into his flesh.

She heard Frank running back. She did not know how long he had been but she knew that Mason had eight minutes before becoming brain dead.

'It's not there!' Frank said. 'Someone's bloody nicked it!'

This was an old story in the prison. 'Have you got a knife?' she said.

Mason's eyes were rolling backwards into his head.

'Just a penknife.' He gave it to her.

The blade was covered in dark stains from sharpening pencils. She felt it. It was sharp.

'Turn him over.'

Frank turned him over so that the back of his head was towards them. She cut quickly with a downward stroke just above the tight cord. The blade sank into the flesh and blood spurted. She felt the blade meet the hempen cord. She began to saw at it. In a second or two it flew apart. They turned him over again.

'Oh God!' she said.
'Are we too late?' Frank said.
'Yes, I think we are.'

26

My love, it was something Mr Watchman ate. I thought the pork sounded indigestible when the Judge told me. Anyway he can't come, not this evening. Just as well I didn't give him your glove, isn't it? I'm still not sure about him. I mean who really knows what these people from Africa think and do? But on the other hand they may have a kind of knowledge we don't have.

Lily has the glove in her hand and is looking out at the grey sky through Sandra's bedroom window.

Did I tell you Peter phoned again? Oh, yes. And would I have dinner with him? I asked him here to supper but he says I'm not to cook. He wants to take me to the Castle Hotel in Kingstown on Saturday night. I haven't been there for years.

It's very good nowadays, they say, with a French chef and everything. So I said yes please that would be lovely. I think I'm going to buy myself a new suit. Remember that dark green one I had? The one with the black collar? Something like that. I've got nothing for an occasion. Only there never have seemed to be any occasions. And I'm going to have my hair done. I've made the appointment. There's a new place just off the square that people say is good. Oh, and Olive said would I consider helping her in the shop a couple of days a week? She's got a back problem and she wants to have the time to go and see a physio. So I said why not? It'll make me a few pounds.

She holds the glove up to her cheek and thinks for a moment she smells Sandra's smell.

I'll go down now, she says.

She tucks the glove into the pocket of her cardigan and as she does so she realises that she carries it everywhere now. She has done so without any conscious plan. It has just happened.

She closes Sandra's bedroom door and goes down to the living-room and checks the programmes in a TV magazine. There is a soap in ten minutes which she has enjoyed in the past. She thinks she'll watch it.

She is putting the magazine down on the couch when she hears the voice again. It says:

Find me!

Oh, God, Sandra, is it you? Have I heard you again? Oh, my love, we've tried, we have really tried. It's not my fault so many people are giving up.

It comes again and this time she is frightened. Is it what she thought she had avoided? Is it madness?

But recently she'd been with more people than ever before, even when Barry was alive. Surely they would have noticed and surely she would have guessed what they were thinking?

But Sandra wants her. Sandra needs to be found!
I'm coming, my love, I'm coming . . .

She was in her rubber boots and her mackintosh.
The light was going and she did not really want to
be out but Sandra wanted it and she wanted what
Sandra wanted. If some people needed to mourn,
other people needed to be found.

She went quickly up the gallops. A young man,
one of the new villagers, was coming down with a
dog.

'Evening,' he said. 'Looks like rain.'

She nodded and was past him in a moment.

She reached the level plain with the river on
one side of it and the woods on the other. The place
looked dreadful. The tapes had been blown about
in the wind. Some members of the last working
party must have brought cans of lager and Coke
and thrown the empties on the ground. There were
also chocolate wrappers and banana skins. She was
glad Elizabeth Drayton had not come out and seen
what was happening to her land.

Lily touched the glove in her pocket. 'Not that
she keeps it well herself,' she said to Sandra. 'All
the weeds and the broken fences. Not like it used
to be.' She walked along the river bank then swung
inland. 'Where my love? Where should I search?'

She had no confidence in walking along the tapes.
Why would anyone bury someone here in the middle
of a 'set-aside' field? She made for the wood.

'This would be the place,' she said to Sandra. 'All the leaf mould and the dane-holes. This is where I'd have come, although it's a long way from the Chittys' place.'

She took her time, criss-crossing the soft and spongy earth where she had not walked before. There was a strong smell of decaying leaves which reminded her of fresh mushrooms. She spent half an hour in the thicket and the light went quickly, for the trees had their new spring leaves and cut off the area from the surrounding meadowland and from the sky.

Sandra's glove was in her hand and she rubbed it occasionally on her cheek as though to make contact with her daughter.

She pushed at light branches that blocked her path. 'Are you here, my love?'

The wool of the glove snagged a branch and she decided to put it away. Sandra must know she was there.

As she felt for her anorak pocket she dropped the glove and an eddy of wind caught it and whisked it away a couple of yards. It teetered on the edge of a dane-hole and then fell into it.

Lily stood on the edge of the hole. It was one of several on Mrs Drayton's land where lumps of flint had been dug out by farmers. Some had been dug for weapons in prehistoric times and during the Danelaw, but more recently for building material. This hole was about half the size of a tennis court and about four feet deep. It had been used as a dump for old silage bales in their black plastic coverings. Most were torn and had spilled their contents. It wasn't the most pleasant spot.

Lily climbed down carefully and retrieved Sandra's glove. She was straightening up when a voice said, 'What the hell do you want?'

Samuel Chitty was standing above her. His face was angry and he had a shotgun in his hands.

'What I want's got nothing to do with you,' Lily said.

'I differs on that. You'd better tell me.'

'You know exactly what I want. You've been watching us ever since we started. I'm looking for my daughter's body and you aren't going to stop me.'

'I told you before to stay away.'

His dark eyes and thin, dark face hovered above her like ectoplasm.

'What?'

'You heard me!'

'But this isn't your land! It's Mrs Drayton's land!'

He looked nonplussed for a moment. Then his face knotted with rage and he raised the shotgun barrel.

'Clear off!'

'Why?'

'Because I'm telling you!'

'Why are you saying this? It's not your business why I'm here.'

'I've made it my business. We doesn't want you interfering.'

'I'm not interfering. She's my daughter! And you should be helping to find her. It was your brother that murdered her. I want her buried. I want to mourn; to grieve. And you come and threaten me and tell me to get off a place that isn't yours. It's you that's interfering. You that's . . .' She stopped suddenly. 'Oh, my God! You know where she is, don't you, Samuel? She's somewhere here, isn't she? You know where Mason put her!'

'I want you gone!'

'That's why you've been watching us. And it was *you* who hit that old black man in the face. He was getting too close, wasn't he? You didn't want us to find her. You and that mother of yours were always secretive. The most secretive people in the village. But what do you care about Mason? You never cared a jot before so why do you want to stop me finding her? It won't make it any better for you and your mother because the police *know* he did it. They don't *need* the body.'

Then suddenly a thought hit so hard it almost caused her to fall. 'Oh . . .' she said, 'Oh my God . . . it wasn't Mason, was it? It was you! *You're* the one. You killed my Sandra!'

His eyes seemed to enlarge. His face was dark red. He said, 'She was a bloody whore. She deserved to die.'

She began to pull herself up the side of the dane-

298

hole. He shifted the gun to his shoulder and she stopped.

'Are you going to kill me now?' she shouted. 'D'you think I care? What have I to live for? Pull the trigger!'

She could see that it was in his mind and she *didn't* care.

And then the shadow of a tree behind him turned into something else. A dark shape. It moved towards them. Branches bent and snapped. She could see Samuel's face change as he registered that someone was there. He turned. Swung the gun, stepped back one pace, and his foot slid down the side of the dane-hole. He dropped the gun.

He fell sprawling across the plastic silage bales. She saw his face become congealed with horror and his eyes fill with terror. The black bale had torn under his weight and he was staring at the skeletal bones of a hand and arm.

'Oh, God!' she cried.

He turned and began to lever himself up.

'You bastard!' She raised her torch and hit him. She hit him on his temple. He groaned and tried to snatch the torch. She hit him in the face. He came up onto his knees and got to his feet. The gun was within his reach. He grabbed for it but the jellied mass in the plastic bale heaved under his weight and he slipped and fell. Lily scrambled up the side of the hole, slid, fell back, groped in the leaf mould for purchase then gripped a root and pulled herself up.

She ran into the scrub but heard Samuel come after her. The branches held her. She fought them. There were too many. She turned. He was a few yards behind her, fumbling at the safety catch of the gun but it was covered with slime and mud. She turned and hit him again. He groaned and tried to aim the gun. She hit him again and again. She went on hitting him after he had fallen until she could hit him no longer.

She was crying and her body was shaking. The torch was still in her hand, the big, black, heavy Mag-lite torch which Barry had given her. It was dented and bloody and the head it had hit was also dented and bloody.

His body lay in the dense undergrowth and she was standing over it when Watch caught up with her. This was not the time for her to talk, not the time for explanations, and by the terrified expression on his face she knew it was not the time for him either.

'I'll wait here,' she said. 'Please go down to Mrs Drayton's and phone for the police.'

There was something she had to do and she had to do it alone.

When she was sure he had gone she went back to the dane-hole. The skeletal hand was just visible if you knew where to look and she was certain that Mr Watchman would not have seen it. She climbed down again onto the silage bales and began to pull them over the one in which Sandra lay. She piled them on top and then she broke open several and spread their soggy contents about the hole as though animals had broken into the bales. She worked until the very shape of the dane-hole had changed.

Then she walked back to where Samuel's body lay in the thicket and waited for the police.

27

'You haven't won the lottery without telling me?' Anne was reading a restaurant menu and her eyebrows were raised.

Tom said, 'You're not to look at the prices.'

'Really?'

'Yes, really. I've been wanting to take you to dinner for God knows how long and I'll be angry if you even glance at them. In fact, let me order for you. Do you like lobster? The thermidor is excellent.'

'I love it.'

They were in a small restaurant in Bathurst Street off the Bayswater Road in London. It was Tom's choice and he had told her that Pip, the chef, was a Paris-trained South Vietnamese who cooked fish like no one else.

'What about the oysters to start with?'

'Oysters, then lobster thermidor. What have I done to deserve this?'

'What you've done is get the whole lot of us off the hook. If you hadn't saved Mason I shudder to think what would have happened.'

'You need to thank Frank for that too. If he hadn't had that knife we'd have lost Mason. I thought we had at first.'

'The TV and the newspapers would have taken us apart. Two innocent men in a row committing suicide would have been horrendous. By the way what's going to happen to Mason?'

'He's taken over the farm and he's bought a house for his adoptive mother in Kingstown. He may be all right.'

They had driven to London after the inquest into the death of Samuel Chitty had come to an end earlier that day.

Tom said, 'Inquests are unsatisfactory in many ways. I mean they don't tell us what happened, they just make vague noises of unhappiness with situations. What do you think really happened?'

'I think it's what we hear often enough from our own prisoners. They commit a crime, then they are overwhelmed by thoughts that people are suspicious of them, then they commit another crime in an attempt to hide the first. Samuel must have been watching people coming and going past his gate, along his fences, in the adjoining valley. It's easy enough to see he must have felt psychotic about the search parties. And suddenly something snapped.'

'Mrs Benson was lucky your Mr Watch was there. Chitty would have killed her all right. What was he doing there anyway? I thought he'd eaten something that made him ill; didn't you tell me it was stuffed lamb?'

'Pork. Father had stuffed it with paté. Can you

304

imagine anything richer? Anyway, Watch being a mountain man had decided to walk off his feeling of nausea and he'd driven in father's car to the one place he knew. But father thinks there's more to it than that. He thinks Watch wanted to prove his powers or even that he had perceived an aura about that place — if that's what you do with auras. Anyhow, he was in the right place at the right time. In fact it was close to the spot where he was cracked on the nose. And his evidence clears Lily of murdering Samuel Chitty. My father says it's a clear case of self-defence.'

'How is your father? I want to keep abreast of the man I'm supposed to be like.'

She laughed. 'Fine. He needs having things to worry and brood about and he's got something new now: the Future and his part in it.'

'I thought his future was running the house and looking after you and Hilly.'

'Not any more.'

The oysters came and she said, 'Do you mind if I don't talk for a while? I haven't had oysters for ages. And a whole dozen! Don't they look wonderful.'

She ate the oysters and drank Chablis and then she told him what had changed her domestic arrangements.

She had woken one morning and heard what she thought were strange noises coming from the kitchen. Usually her father woke early and made the breakfast for the three of them. But these sounds seemed more subdued and organised than the clatter and bang she was used to. She slipped on a dressing-gown and went down and there was Watch in the middle of the kitchen, neatly dressed in grey flannels and a white shirt with a blue-and-white butcher's apron round his waist.

'Good morning, Watch. What's this?' she had said.

And he had replied in a tone of voice she had not heard for a long time, 'Blekfas in one hour.'

'But you shouldn't be doing this, you're a guest here, you're on holiday.'

He had fixed her with a piercing eye and said, 'I cannot eat any more of the Judge's cooking. If I do I will eh-pass away.'

He gave her a cup of tea and she was whirled back in time to the red sand-dunes of the Kalahari and the winter snows of the Maluti Mountains in Lesotho. He had managed by some sleight of hand to make the tea taste of Africa.

She went up to wake Hilly and wondered what Watch would give them for breakfast. She knew she would have to tell him that they no longer ate eggs, bacon, sausages, fried bread, kidneys and lamb chops.

'And what did he say when you told him?' Tom said.

'He was perfectly adaptable. Much more so than my father. And then he said he was taking Hilly to school, which he did. The house is now running like clockwork.'

'What happens when he goes back to wherever it was he came from?'

'The word is *if* not *when.*'

The lobster came. Again there was silence. Anne finished and licked her fingers. 'That was marvellous.'

Tom sat back with the wine glass in his hand and said, 'And Sandra's murder? What's the scenario on that one?'

'No one will ever know for certain. I went to see Lily but she doesn't want to talk about it and I can't say I blame her. I think Mason did have a fight with Sandra. He may even have injured her. He says he can't remember what happened and I'm sure that's right because he really thought he'd killed her. He probably knocked her down and then left the stables. Samuel found her there.'

'Why wasn't he a suspect?'

'He was a taxi-driver in Kingstown at the time, with his own cab. He could go anywhere he liked and no one would have known. Mason said he didn't think Samuel followed him that day, but Samuel must have come out to the farm for some reason, seen the two of them go into the stables and that was that. According to Mitchell and Betty Sugden he'd been trying to get at Sandra for a long time. They said she hated him. Called him a peasant. Ironic isn't it? And Mason said Samuel always destroyed his possessions. In this case Sandra was one of them.' She paused. 'The whole thing's a bizarre moral tale really.'

'Oh? You could have fooled me.'

'All right, an ironic bizarre moral tale then. According to some of the people I talked to, Lily Benson was living a lonely and rather miserable life. Then her daughter is killed and the body hidden and because Lily sets out to find Sandra her life changes. She meets people, goes out, entertains.'

Tom said, 'I can see the irony all right. But do you think she has taken on board the reality of her daughter?'

'God knows. The evidence at the inquest was pretty specific about Sandra. But parents, and especially mothers, see the best in their children. Don't forget we have them from birth when they're completely innocent and everything that happens to them later, all their adult characteristics, are built on this memory of innocence.'

'You sound like Donne or Herrick, but I wonder if it's as simple as that.'

'My father says she must have known what her own daughter was like before all this happened. I suppose she might have buried it in her subconscious. People do.'

It was nearly midnight when they left London. The journey was dominated by the return of the familiar tension. Anne had guessed it would come but they had been so relaxed in the restaurant that she had not thought of it. Now as they drove through Surrey the journey was punctuated by sudden bursts of conversation as each felt the silence grow embarrassing.

In one of those silences Anne said, 'What do you hear of Stephanie?'

The moment she said it she wished she hadn't because it reminded her of her own abrupt behaviour to Tom.

'She's in London,' he said. Then after a moment he went on, 'She's still phoning me. Not so often but once a week.'

'Still the same reason?'

'Still the same. The problem is that every time I hear her voice I think she's going to say she's overdosed again. I know it's blackmail, but what the hell can one do?'

He pulled up outside her house.

She said, 'I still feel bloody about turning on you the way I did.'

'Don't give it another thought, I haven't?' He put his hand on her arm.

Perhaps it was some tactile sense but whatever it was she knew right away that she wanted him. The evening had been celebratory. It had been fun. It needed an ending. (He's your boss, her other voice said.)

'I'd ask you up for coffee,' she said, 'but I'd wake the household.' That was a lie and he probably knew it but she didn't care. 'Is there any place that's open now?'

'In Kingstown? You must be joking.'

She knew this was a rather old-fashioned conversation and that the feminist way was a straightforward: I'd like to fuck you. She didn't think she could manage the feminist way, so she went on like someone in a 1950s Ealing comedy.

'I could really do with a coffee,' she said.

'There's always my place.'

'So there is.'

He leaned forward to start the car and a voice called, 'Mummy! Mummy!'

Anne looked up at the house and in a lighted window saw Hilly. She put down the car window and said, 'Hello, darling. Why aren't you asleep?'

'I woke up. Mr Watch has been reading to me.'

Anne turned to Tom. 'I'll take a raincheck on the coffee if I may.'

'A real raincheck?'

'Yes, a real raincheck.'

She leaned over and kissed him on the cheek. Under the gaze of her small daughter it was what Lily Benson might have called a Christmas kiss.

It's all over, my love. The inquest's over and the police have finished with me.

Lily is near the dane-hole. Not very near, in case people are watching, but near enough to see what's what. The sun has come out and she leans against a tree letting the warmth envelop her body. To her right an old overgrown logging track winds into the trees in the direction of the Downs. It is the way, she thinks, that Samuel brought Sandra down on his tractor; just a black bale on the lifting fork; so easy. She will never know for certain. But she doesn't care now how Sandra got there; as long as she knows where she is.

The torn black plastic bales and the old silage which burst from them have formed a kind of covering, a carapace, in the hole. Each time she comes this way, and she comes three or four times a week, she throws soil and leaf mould on top of them. She has a small packet of grass seed in her anorak pocket and she broadcasts it by hand. Already grass is beginning to sprout.

And the smell is going. The smell of rotting silage.

Of course, I had to throw away my clothes, my love. Did you hear me say, 'of course'? That's Peter. I see quite a lot of him. Not bad for a lieutenant's wife, is it? Sometimes I tell myself I'll be the next Lady Pattinson, but I know deep down that I won't. No matter, I enjoy him. And I enjoy going up to see Elizabeth Drayton and I enjoy having a drink with the Judge and Mr Watchman. And I enjoy working in the shop and talking to everyone there.

And looking for you, of course. Peter and I still look. And occasionally some of the others. The Kingstown paper has been out to interview me about the search and there's talk of a TV programme.

I wonder if they think I'm mad to go on searching as I do. But, you see, once we find you a great many

311

things may come to an end and we can't have that, can we?

My love, I can't stay today. They've asked me to collect books for the Save the Children Fund's fête, so I must get on with it.

So goodbye, my darling, I'll talk to you tomorrow. No . . . not tomorrow. Peter and I are going to see the Mary Rose *at Portsmouth. It'll be so interesting seeing an historic ship with an admiral on hand to explain everything. He spent years in Portsmouth, you know. Oh, yes, years . . .*

She has not walked more than a hundred yards from the grave when the voice in her head says: Bitch!

She stops for a moment.

There was a time when she would have been frozen with fright, when she would have been certain she was going mad.

Not now.

Now there is only a deep sadness inside her, for she knows this is not Sandra's voice but a voice that comes from a box owned by all parents and marked, 'Where did I go wrong?'

The voice is her own.